BACK AT LAST

SERENDIPITY BOOK THREE

BACK AT
LAST

KT BOND

4 Horsemen
Publications, Inc.

Back at Last
Serendipity Series Book 3
Copyright © 2023 KT Bond. All rights reserved.

4 Horsemen
Publications, Inc.

4 Horsemen Publications, Inc.
1497 Main St. Suite 169
Dunedin, FL 34698
4horsemenpublications.com
info@4horsemenpublications.com

Cover by Ron Perry Graphic Design, rperrydesign.com
Typesetting by Autumn Skye
Editor CI Stearns

Library of Congress Control Number: 2022949769

Paperback ISBN-13: 978-1-64450-719-3
Hardcover ISBN-13: 978-1-64450-833-6
Ebook ISBN-13: 978-1-64450-720-9
Audio ISBN-13: 978-1-64450-834-3

TABLE OF
CONTENTS

PROLOGUE

Why the devil can't I keep my eyes off her?
Rory Stewart turned away from the woman he'd caught himself staring at again to smile at Peter van der Meulen, to whom he'd been introduced earlier. He was Karen's husband ... Karen, Antonia Larson's best friend and matron of honor at her wedding. He nodded when Peter said the little chapel was exquisitely decorated.

"It is indeed," he said, needing to force himself to focus on the man standing next to him instead of on the woman across the aisle currently doing her level best to ignore him as hard as he was trying to ignore her.

"Have you known the couple long?" Peter asked in his very formal way.

At any other time, Rory might have found Peter's almost staid demeanor a bit boring, but at this moment, he welcomed the older man's gently meandering conversation. Anything was better than letting his gaze wander back over to where Christina Marcus sat, eyes straight ahead, apparently engrossed in observing the pianist playing melodious tunes with great skill and enthusiasm.

"I've only known Niall since Toni met him, but I've known Toni for a while, yes."

"They are very well suited," Peter opined with a contented smile.

Rory knew the story behind that smile. There had been a time when Peter had worried that he'd have to fight to win his now-wife's regard away from the hunky man Toni was marrying today. You didn't have to like men to see that Niall McLaren was a gorgeous male specimen. Rory had known *he* hadn't stood a chance against the other man for Toni's affection when he'd shown up at that party a year ago. He'd also only known Niall since that fateful night when he'd met Chrissy for the first time ... good Lord, there he was again, thinking about a woman who wanted nothing to do with him.

Taking a deep breath, he forced himself to initiate a new thread of conversation. If he had to, he'd talk about the bloody weather before he let himself spend another second thinking about Chrissy.

"Toni and Karen have apparently been friends for a while, as well. Some people do manage to keep their friendships intact for ages, don't they?" *Way to sound like a blithering idiot, Ro!*

Peter turned curious eyes to his face. "Some do, yes. Are you not one of them?"

Rory considered the question. "I suppose I am, although the nature of *my* long-standing friendships is somewhat less deep than what appears to be between your wife and Toni." And wasn't that a pitiful truth!

Before Peter could reply, the pianist ended the song she'd been playing, shuffled her music sheets, and looked over at the door behind the guests. Rory followed her gaze and saw that the wedding party was assembled, all awaiting their musical cue. A youthful male cellist and two female violinists who had been sitting in the front row, also waiting for the moment to arrive, joined the pianist. Pachelbel's "Canon" began its stately round as the men and women walked up the aisle together. The women were elegant in their pale blue tea-length satin dresses, the men in gray morning suits, shirts the same color as the women's dresses, and cream ties. After they were all in position, the four musicians heralded the arrival of the parents of the bride and groom to the sounds of a lively piece by Handel.

When the full orchestral recording of the opening strains of the traditional "Bridal Chorus" from *Lohengrin* by Richard Wagner sounded, Rory rose with the other guests and turned to watch his friend and her soon-to-be-husband making their stately way together down the aisle to the front. He was not surprised that his friend had chosen to walk down the aisle on Niall's arm instead of on her father's, and he loved that she also chose to walk to the original choral version of the popular piece.

The orchestral and choral sounds provided a majestic background against which the bride and groom appeared, smiling adoringly at each other before beginning their walk to where the others stood waiting for them. Toni looked radiant in her creamy vintage lace and satin dress, and the smile on her face was echoed by the one creasing her groom's cheeks as he held her tenderly. Rory wondered idly as they passed him how long it would take Niall to undo the many buttons on the back of Toni's dress once he got her alone later.

If it were him, he'd likely pop off every one of them in an effort to get to the woman beneath them. His mind followed the path of a wedding night he honestly didn't expect to ever enjoy himself, and the woman he had managed not to think about for the last ten minutes snapped back onto his mental screen. He glanced over at her as the music died away and found her gaze on him.

Chrissy was a sight for sore eyes. Small, deliciously curvy, pretty—she was everything he had spent the last six months trying to forget—dressed in a one-shoulder, three-quarter-sleeved yellow sheath dress with bold satin draped over the right shoulder. She wore her now-abundant hair up in an elegant do held together by a pretty silk ribbon the same color as her dress. She made him smile, even as he struggled to remember why he should not be smiling at her. *With* her, because she returned it with one of her own, tentative, perhaps hopeful, a kind of truce in their six-month-long standoff.

"Ladies and gentlemen, please take your seats."

Rory pulled his gaze away from the tantalizing woman. He hadn't come to see her, though he suspected that she'd be there, since she and Toni were not only friends but co-workers. He refocused his attention on the proceedings at the front of the chapel, enjoying—as he always did at these events—the familiarity of traditional vows, the beauty of the classical music, and the delightful elegance of the entire experience. He might not think he'd ever marry, but he loved weddings and everything they stood for, despite his own history.

No thinking about that today either, Ro. This isn't about you. Once more pulling his thoughts away from the dark place they had been headed toward, he watched as Niall kissed Toni. It was a sweet, somewhat steamy kiss, not long enough to raise any eyebrows but definitely making a statement. One that Rory found himself remembering wanting to make all those years ago. Another lifetime, it felt like, and he'd never go there again, especially not after...

Mendelssohn's joyous "Wedding March" began, and Rory sighed in relief. He really needed to get a grip. He wasn't a teenager, for goodness' sake! He was a grown man. He had to stop getting lost in his head over nonsense he neither had any control over nor wanted to entertain. As the little chapel emptied itself of the small group of guests, he waited his turn to follow the party out, smiling pleasantly at anyone who met his eye. Eventually, he found himself outside on the quiet front lawn of the church.

"Aren't you Riordan?"

Rory looked around to see who had spotted him. He hadn't thought too much about his other persona because he'd been so engrossed in thoughts of Chrissy and of the wedding. But he was, after all was said and done, a rockstar. It would have been unusual had he not been recognized. He smiled at the boy who stood next to him, eyeing him with a kind of wonder that he found strangely endearing.

"I am," he replied simply. "And you are?"

"I'm Joshua Buchanan. Where's your band? And your bodyguard?" He looked around as though he expected them to jump out from the hedges.

Rory chuckled. "The others weren't invited," he explained. "And my bodyguard was relieved of his duties for the day. Don't worry, I'm safe. Mr. McLaren is looking after me."

The boy studied him for a moment, then said, "Yeah, Uncle Niall is cool."

Ah, Niall's nephew. Rory didn't know any of the groom's family, and he had only heard of Toni's brothers in passing but hadn't met any of *them*, either. He smiled.

"He is, isn't he? I mean, only a cool guy like your uncle would be lucky enough to find such a lovely lady to marry."

The boy grinned easily, and then sobered just as quickly. "I'd better go before Mum comes to get me. She told us not to disappear."

He turned to hurry away, then turned back to add, "Nice to meet you, sir."

Rory chuckled again as the boy scurried off to find his mother and whoever else she had warned not to disappear. He couldn't remember ever being called 'sir' before, and it tickled his funny bone at the same time that it settled a new and melancholy feeling in his chest. Only his father, Sir Edmund Riordan Stewart, II, was called sir. He had only that morning addressed him as such in their brief but decidedly uncomfortable conversation. He wouldn't dwell on that now, however. This was a wedding, and he was meant to be enjoying himself.

He turned to follow the other guests out to the car park. He was looking forward to the reception where he could reconnect with Toni, meet her handsome new husband, and forget for a while that he was actually lonely. Seeing Chrissy again had derailed his control, but he'd been lonely long enough to be a past master at controlling the feeling. He would deal with it the way he had everything else so far ... with a warm smile and a cool heart.

CHAPTER 1

"Director Hayes' office, good morning. How may I help you?"

Chrissy listened patiently while the caller explained why his needs couldn't be met by anyone other than her immediate boss and then let him down gently.

"I'm sorry, sir, but the director is unavailable at the moment. She's in a meeting with the board of directors. If you'll leave me your contact information, I'll be sure to get it to her. She will return your call as soon as she's able."

After she hung up, she added to the list of calls on her boss's digital calendar, then went back to the report she'd been typing. She had two more to complete by the time Anna James's meeting ended, and she needed to be ready for the next influx of reports and phone calls that she'd be required to make. Her job as executive assistant to the director of Hope House was challenging, even on the best days. And today was going to be a long day, if the number of meetings her boss had scheduled was any indicator. It was a good thing she had come in an hour earlier to get going. She couldn't allow herself to get behind, because while Dr. James was not a cruel boss, she was exacting and could be impatient.

Chrissy had had enough emotional upheaval to last her a while, thank you very much. Seeing Rory Stewart again the past weekend had been harder to deal with than she'd thought it would be when Toni had told her that she had invited him to her wedding. He was as handsome as he'd always been, blond and golden and gorgeous in every way. He looked like the rockstar he was, despite his attempts to hide that glamour behind the bespoke morning suit that he wore. It was clear to her that he was a man of wealth and power, as well as a rockstar in his own right. The way he'd looked at the wedding—toned, tanned, and delicious—was what made him irresistible to all the groupies who crowded around the band after each of his shows.

Don't go there, C! She pulled her thoughts away from Rory. She wasn't being paid to moon over a man who made his living making women swoon over his words and his voice and his gorgeous self. When the meeting ended, Dr. James would return and expect that the arrangements she'd made for luncheon in the large conference room were complete, and that her lunch guests knew where to go. She didn't have time for dilly-dallying. Saving the final document before sending it for review, she stood, taking her tablet with her to go to the conference room.

Dr. James had chosen to host the luncheon here instead of at the restaurant they usually used, but the food was being catered by them, and they had already begun to set up when she walked in. She smiled at the men as they moved around, changing the space to look more like a dining room and less like the conference room that it was. Dr. James had insisted on keeping the design fluid, which meant Japanese-style screens on two sides to remove the enormous widescreen television and the whiteboards from view. The pristine white tablecloth, atop a heavy table pad, covered the large conference table, which also had laptop portals that slid beneath its surface for such occasions as these.

She stood to the side, watching as they positioned the chafing dishes and then the pans of hot food. Things seemed to be well in hand. She checked her watch ... twenty minutes until lunch. She approached the man who was clearly in charge—a small, elegant fellow with a streak of purple in his ash-blond hair—smiling and extending her hand.

"Jean-Paul, everything looks wonderful, as expected."

The sous chef smiled. "You know Michel only puts his best foot forward for Dr. James. He would have come himself but he's fighting a nasty bug. And I can't stay, but we've given you our best interns."

He turned to look at the two young men finishing the setup and checking that everything they needed was in place.

"Michel and I will probably hire them once their final term in cooking school is over. It would be a shame to lose them."

Chrissy knew that that was high praise indeed coming from one of the premier chefs in the city.

"I'm sure everything will be fine," she returned with a smile. "I'll have the balance in your account shortly. And please give my best to Michel. I hope he gets better soon."

Jean-Paul nodded and walked over to give his team final instructions before leaving, sending her a wave as he did so. Chrissy's phone rang, the call showing up on her tablet. She answered, stepping over to the window away from the food being set out and the men working quietly to get things done by the time the diners arrived.

"Yes, Dr. James?"

"Are you ready for us, Christine?"

Her boss never called her by her nickname. She was a stickler for formality whenever it could be preserved, and it was as much as she would do not to call Chrissy "Ms. Marcus."

"Yes, Boss. Everything is ready when you are."

"Very well. We'll be there shortly."

Chrissy waited only long enough for Dr. James and the seven men and women on the board to file in before she made her escape. She'd probably go out for lunch today since these board luncheons usually went on longer than usual. Toni was on her honeymoon, so Chrissy wouldn't have a companion for the meal as she normally did, but she was used to being alone, so she ignored the niggle of loneliness that spiked as she walked out into the midday sunshine. The day was cheerful, and the walk to the little bistro where she and Toni sometimes ate helped to lift her spirits. It was as crowded as usual, but she managed to find a table for two in the tiny but bright back garden. Ordering her usual—a hot ham and cheese sandwich with pickles and onions, a small green salad, and a pitcher of water—she let her mind go back to the wedding reception where she had seen Rory again for the first time in six months.

She had noticed him the minute he'd walked into the little chapel. Something in the air had announced the arrival of someone distinguished, and she hadn't needed to turn her head to know that. He sat in the seat across from hers, a blond lock falling in a perfect coil over his left eye as always. He flicked it away with a careless slide of his fingers, and she'd watched, as fascinated as she had been from that first time seeing him at her birthday party, as the lock of hair slowly inched its way back down the golden slide to his forehead. She wanted to sink her fingers into its soft length, to luxuriate in the decadent feel of it.

They'd done their best to avoid looking at each other throughout the service, and after, she'd been torn between relief and disappointment that they hadn't been seated together. She'd been at a table with Toni's other workmates who had been invited, while Rory sat with people Chrissy didn't know, except for Karen's husband, whom she'd met when the couple had come over for a visit and been in to see Toni at work. Afterwards, though, when you could sit wherever you chose, she'd ended up next to him, and they had been forced to be sociable.

She understood why a man like Rory—any man, in all honesty—might be angry with her and treat her badly as a result. They'd gone on a few dates after her birthday party, where she'd found out who he was and what he did for a living. As the lead singer and main lyricist for the rock band Third Generation, he'd been everything she imagined such a man would be ... brimming with talent and charisma and an undeniable sex appeal. She'd been attracted to him from the moment she'd seen him at her party and was secretly overjoyed when he'd agreed to escort her home.

"Thanks for the ride," she'd said when they got to her flat. "I appreciate it."

His smile had warmed her. "It was my pleasure, Christine. I hope you enjoyed your party. Welcome to the thirties."

They'd laughed together at that, and she'd been bold enough to ask him how old he was.

"I assume also in your thirties," she added as an explanation for her temerity.

In truth, he didn't look his age. He had told her he was thirty-seven, but he didn't look a day older than she was. He had the sort of face that defied aging, that seemed to speak of a kind of youthful *joie de vivre*. His blond locks looked almost golden in the roof light when she opened the car door, and his blue eyes sparkled with warmth.

"You've got some good genes there," she'd teased. "I'll be thrilled to look as good as you when I'm your age."

His laughter had filled the car, relieving her mind because immediately the words had left her lips, she'd cringed at all the things wrong with them. She hadn't meant to imply that he was an old man, and she definitely hadn't wanted to let on how attractive she found him. So it was a good thing he found her amusing instead of annoying and even insulting.

"Thanks." He'd gotten out of the car then and walked around just as she was getting out herself. "I'll walk you to your door."

Such a gentleman! She rented the garden flat in a townhouse in a quiet section of the city, and she loved how private it was. She enjoyed her independence, especially now that she was not only living alone but also doing so hours away from the place where she had spent most of her life. She loved her aunts and would be forever grateful for their intervention in her life when she had been a newborn and most vulnerable. But she had known she would never follow in their footsteps and become a nun, and the lifestyle in which she had been raised had done enough to teach her how to be safe on her own in London.

"This garden must be really pretty in daylight," Rory had remarked as they walked through the garden gate around to where her front entrance was.

"It is, and now that the forsythia is in bloom, it's also a little shady as well."

"May I take you out for a drink sometime?" he'd asked as she rummaged in her purse for her key.

Even now, despite the state of their relationship—well, non-relationship, really, since she and he were still not seeing each other—the memory of the way she'd felt when he asked to see her again held a warm, quiet sweetness. Even if he didn't feel the spark that she felt at his nearness, at least he was interested enough to want to meet again. She'd given him her phone so he could add his number, and when a text message arrived a moment later, she'd added him to her contacts.

She finished lunch without paying much attention to what she ate. Thinking about Rory always made her lose track of time, and if her aunt Zelda were around, she'd be the first to tell her that that was a sign that he was important, and that she shouldn't ignore it. Aunt Zelda, or Auntie ZeeZee as Chrissy used to call her, was the one of twin sisters who had sown a whole lot of wild oats before deciding that a life dedicated to the service of others in the name of Christ was how she was meant to live.

Thinking of them reminded her that she needed to call her aunts. They had long since given up trying to persuade her that living and working in the same city where they lived and worked, even if she moved into her own space, was what would be best for her. The other twin aunt, Sister Mary Clare, had been especially indignant when Chrissy had first broached the subject of moving to London to work. She had put forth every argument she could think of to convince Chrissy that remaining in Ely was best. Aunt Clare was by far the more introverted and cautious of the twins and had been a nun for all her adult life, so Chrissy understood her reluctance to give her seal of approval. A move to London was a much bigger deal to her than it was to Aunt Zelda. She would call them when she got home later.

The rest of her day was filled with the usual business of being the executive assistant to the director of an organization that worked to support and care for battered and abused women and their families. Finally, thankfully, Chrissy shut down her laptop, pleased with all that she'd managed to accomplish before it was time to call it quits for the day. Tomorrow would be a full day again, what with the influx of new clients set to arrive. Because Toni was away, Chrissy would complete some of the intake work, thus freeing the remaining social workers to do the parts she couldn't do. But she'd think about that when the time came. For now, she needed to get home to the two cats she'd adopted. She would call her aunts while she fed them and herself.

"I'm fine, Aunt Clare. How are you doing?" she asked an hour later, as she scraped food into the cats' bowls and watched them both swish their tails as they enjoyed their dinner.

"I'm fighting a bit of a cold, dear," her aunt said, her voice rusty with the evidence. "And your aunt Zelda is quite under the weather as well." A sneeze interrupted her aunt's words, and Chrissy listened as she blew her nose before continuing. "Sorry."

"Oh dear, you really don't sound well, Auntie," Chrissy said, suddenly worried about her older relatives. "I'll come for a visit this weekend. Unless you need me before? I can ask for a couple of days off to come and help you both."

It wouldn't be ideal, and though she knew Dr. James would be more than willing to give her the time away, that would only put more of a burden on someone else, since she was already picking up the slack for Toni. She loved her aunts, and she would do whatever they needed, but she didn't want to make things awkward at work, either. Maybe her aunts were right, and she ought to have stayed in Ely so she'd be close enough to look after them without having to stop working.

"We'd love to have you visit, but it's just not the best time right now."

Chrissy stifled the relief she felt at her aunt's words, and then swallowed the guilt that flared up immediately after. She really needed to work on being a better human being all around. She shouldn't feel relieved that the women who had raised her from the time she was a foundling, who were, in fact, no blood relation to her, were giving her excuses to avoid spending time with them. They loved her. She knew that, and she returned their love with her whole heart and soul. But these days, being with them only seemed to remind her that there was something missing from her life. They had their faith and their passion for the work they did, and she could see how those things made them complete and fulfilled them in ways she envied.

Not that she was unhappy in her job. Professionally, she was content. She had no dreams of greatness, no need for attention beyond what came with the work she did every day. That would only embarrass her. She loved her work at Hope House. The idea that she was participating in even a small way in helping to redirect the lives of the women who passed through their doors filled her with a quiet kind of joy.

But she knew, felt in her bones, that something was missing from her life. An ache beyond mere loneliness consumed the most secret parts of her soul, burrowing into her core. With Rory, she had felt the tangle of emotions begin to unravel. From that first concert, where she'd been given a backstage pass to join the band after the show, she'd seen the two sides of Rory on display. What a night it had been! When the woman laid hands on Rory as he and the band members walked out of the venue after the show, Chrissy had stood by watching in horror.

"Riordan! Can you sign me please?" the fan had screamed, clearly needing to be heard above all the other voices calling out to the band members.

Even now, the remembered shock still shook her. Had the woman really said what Chrissy thought she'd said? How the hell ... *where* the hell was Rory supposed to *sign* her? When the clearly— well, at least now Chrissy realized she was—totally high groupie proceeded to expose a conveniently braless breast, the security guy assigned to him had been immediately in her face, pulling her away while another herded the women who had come with her out of the way.

"No one gets any body parts autographed. If you don't have paper and a pen, you can leave," the band's manager said into the suddenly sub- dued silence. "You all know these guys don't play like that."

Was that something that happened often? Chrissy watched as the men greeted the faithful who hadn't been able to afford the ticket add-on that would have allowed them to meet the band in the green room after the concert. They smiled and posed and signed a few autographs, and she noted how some took every opportunity to sneak touches of their bodies, Rory's in particular. He was very kind to them, flirting gently with the ones who were the least aggressive, a warm smile on his face as he signed albums and whatever else—aside from body parts—that they offered for his signature.

Afterwards, she had felt the spotlight shift from him to her a time or two as he kept her close to his side, stopping every now and again to make sure she was okay, enough that their attention made her uncomfortable.

"Let's get you home," he'd said, turning away to leave with his friends.

A black limousine had pulled up as he spoke, and he opened the door for her. She hadn't missed the wolf whistles that accompanied his gesture and the lewd comments about him getting lucky and hitting it that followed her into the car. Her cheeks flamed as he climbed in on the other side along with the other members of the band.

"Don't mind them, love," the drummer—John—said, smiling at her. "They're crude, but they mean no harm."

She returned his smile, grateful that he was trying to help her feel comfortable. Still, as the vehicle moved off, she couldn't stop the question that popped into her head: what did the rest of the band think about her? She'd only been introduced as a friend of Rory's, and she'd seen the eyebrows raised in question and curiosity and maybe a bit of disbelief. But there had been no real conversation between them. How would she handle anything they might say going forward? They didn't know her any better than she knew them.

"I'm famished," Tristan, the bassist, said. "But I'm not sure I'll be awake long enough to eat."

"I'll believe *that* when I see it," John retorted, making the others laugh with him.

"Shut it, Beats."

Good-natured laughter filled the long car, and Chrissy let Rory pull her closer to his side, loving the warm weight of his arm across her shoulders. She didn't have much in the way of camaraderie like this in her life. She could count the number of her friends on the fingers of one hand, with fingers left over, and there was very little of the comfort of these men's friendship. She was still new in town, still learning her way around, not quite ready to let down the walls she'd put up to protect herself.

Until Rory, she'd only been on a handful of dates, and that was mostly because Toni had nagged her into going. And even with that, she hadn't been out socially with anyone in months. It just took too much effort to put herself out there when she knew after the introductions were done that she had no interest in the man she was with. Was she defective somehow? Because she was pretty sure that she didn't spark any more of an interest in them than they did in her. Or was she deliberately shutting them down because she was unwilling to invest in another human being?

CHAPTER 2

A furball leaning against her heavily brought Chrissy back to the present moment and the flat, which was growing darker as evening rolled in. She needed to make herself something to eat, and apparently, Pickles needed immediate attention. Leaning down, she scratched the cat under his chin and felt the deep purr of pleasure that emanated from his belly, rumbling heavily in his throat.

"You like that, don't you, boy?" she murmured, then chuckled when Lynx came over and butted against her hand, demanding equal attention. Dinner could wait while she showered her pets and only companions with affection.

Half an hour later, both cats having been satisfied with their share of their human's love, Chrissy washed up and headed to the kitchen to see what she could make quickly. There was leftover sweet and sour chicken from the Chinese restaurant, and she could steam some broccoli to go with that and the rest of the rice. The sauce would be a delight on the vegetable. And the last of the apple tarts that she'd bought a few days ago would make a nice dessert with a cup of tea.

Once she'd decided, she quickly prepared her meal and set it on a tray, taking the lot out to the living room, where she sat with her legs up and watched the news while she ate. The story of the capture and arrest of one of Britain's Most Wanted, a man named Randy Richards, filled her mind with disquiet when she heard the crimes of which he was accused. How people could be like that, she would never know.

Growing up as a ward of nuns, she had lived a mostly sheltered life, only approaching anything outside her comfort zone when she volunteered at the children's home where her Aunt Clare was the director. And her experiences were limited to feeding the youngest ones who couldn't—or wouldn't, as it sometimes was—feed themselves and then getting them ready for naptime. She was never told what had brought them to the children's home, but she understood enough to know that their lives had been disrupted by violence against them by adults, some of whom were their parents.

Hope House had given her another wake-up call in the world of human misfortune, and she had vowed never to become one of the women whom she helped to protect and serve there. Which was why she had mostly cut herself off from contact with men ... how was she to know who she could trust, after all? Until Rory came into her life, she had had no reason to suppose that men could be trusted to keep her as safe as she had been able to keep herself thus far.

The shrill ringtone on her phone shook her out of her musings. Reaching for it, she wiped her lips on a napkin and answered.

"This is Chrissy. Good evening. How may I help you?"

"Good evening, Chrissy. It's Rory."

Every single nerve ending in her body sparked to life, zinging at the sound of his light breathing in her ear. As if she wouldn't recognize his voice anywhere!

"Hi, Rory." Why was he calling?

"Hi. How are you?"

Small talk? That wasn't something she remembered about him. He'd always been a straight shooter, making his thoughts and feelings very clear ... except when he wanted to keep them hidden. And he was equally as good at hiding as he was at being seen.

"I'm fine. What's going on?"

She had never mastered small talk either, even though she recognized it, and it made her feel socially awkward to be forced to engage in that way. She also preferred plain speaking ... it was one way to avoid tripping over her tongue. If she didn't try to be coy and seductive or to flirt, she wouldn't embarrass herself ... except when her plain speaking put her in the spotlight in an unflattering way.

"Nothing's going on. I just wondered if you'd like to meet for drinks. I'm still in London for another couple of days and would like to catch up with you."

He paused, the sound of his voice stirring something deep in her belly the way it always did. Did she want to get back in touch as more than wedding guests at a reception? She had asked for time six months ago, had told him she'd be in touch, and then had ghosted him. Why was he trying to hang out with her now? She'd been sure he would never want anything to do with her again after *that* unceremonious parting.

"Ah..." Should she let him down gently, or should she give this a try?

"It's fine if you're not available or interested, Chrissy."

His voice was carefully neutral, with absolutely no inflection, so he was hard to read.

"It's nothing personal, Rory." *Don't be stupid, Christina. Of course it's personal!* She spoke into the awkward silence following her words. "I just thought that after the way things ended six months ago, we had no reason to spend any more time together."

A heavy sigh greeted her words. "Under normal circumstances, I'd be the first to agree with you, Chrissy." He let some feeling she couldn't put a label on leak into his voice this time. "But I've been doing a lot of thinking since the wedding, and a friend has helped me see that if I want a change, I must be willing not only to imagine it but also to initiate it."

She thought she heard footsteps while she waited for him to continue, unsure what *she* could or should say. A muffled curse followed by a quick apology, and then he was speaking again.

"Do you remember what I said to you the first time we went on a date together?"

Would she ever forget? That was probably a better question, but Rory wasn't to know that, was he? Not unless she volunteered that tidbit, and she was very sure she would never share that knowledge with him.

"Yes." Back to monosyllabic responses.

"What did I say?"

Was that a hint of frustration in his voice? What did *he* have to be frustrated about? *She* was the one being tested right now, because he clearly didn't believe she recalled his words.

"You asked me if I was a risk-taker and added that you had to be because of the kind of job you have."

That was certainly no less than the truth. Celebrities like Rory built their lives on the good-will of others, and their reputations made or broke them. Chrissy could never imagine a world in which she would spend as much or more time on the road as she spent at home, at the whim of a career which put her at the mercy of a fickle crowd.

"Why?" She remembered to ask that question before he spoke again.

"Calling you instead of waiting for you to call me, which is what I know you intended when we parted six months ago, is a risk and I know it. But I've also learned over the years that ignoring my gut never pays off."

Chrissy heaved a disbelieving sigh. "So your gut said you should call me?"

"It did."

"And you're prepared to be shot down anyway?" She didn't understand the mindset.

"Risk-taker, remember? So yeah. The worst you can say is no." He paused for a quick second, then added, "So, yes or no, Chrissy?"

Was he manipulating her, or did he really prefer to take a chance on any answer she chose to give? She wanted to stifle her immediate affirmative response, but at the end of the day, what was the point? Seeing him again at the wedding had only made her remember how much she had enjoyed being with him, how deeply he had gotten under her skin, how much she had wanted more with him before she had run away like a scared child.

"Yes." Maybe she needed to become more of a risk-taker herself.

He didn't try to disguise the relief in his voice when he said, "Thank you." If he could be real with her, she owed him no less.

"I'm not making any promises, Rory," she said. "It's just drinks, okay?"

"No pressure, Chrissy. Just drinks, I promise."

"Okay. Well, my schedule hasn't changed, so..."

"I was thinking I'd come by on Saturday evening, if that's okay with you?"

"What time?" She had things to do before she went off gallivanting with a rockstar.

"Eight sound good to you?"

"That's fine. Where are we going?"

"Somewhere I've not taken you before. Casual is fine."

Why was she not surprised that he understood her unspoken question? He'd been intuitive with her from the beginning, and it was one of the things that drew her to him, even as it made her feel vulnerable. Disquiet was not a space she liked to occupy, which was probably why she shied away from starting anything with anyone. Relationships that didn't include calm and sedate emotions were too much for her. She liked order and serenity. Growing up with nuns made that an imperative.

However, something told her that there would never be order and serenity with someone like Rory. So why the hell—*forgive me for swearing, Aunt Clare!*—couldn't she resist him? Their brief time together had been full of laughter and joy, but interspersed between those halcyon moments were others awash in angst and confusion, and on one or two occasions, steeped in disquiet. She never knew from one day to the next where their relationship would take them, and the only constant had been Rory's quiet attention to her needs, even when they were in direct opposition to his desires.

They couldn't work as a couple. They were just too opposite.

"Are you still there, little kitten?"

Unfair! Rory's pet name for her had clearly not lost its powers of seduction, and Chrissy was sure he knew it. Warmth unfurled in her belly at his words, but she forced herself to answer him instead of melting into a puddle of goo the way she usually did. She wouldn't give him the satisfaction of knowing that he still had that power over her.

"Yes. Thank you. I'll be ready at eight on Saturday."

"Excellent. See you then."

She had four days, not counting Saturday. Four days to get her head in the right space to deal with Rory without losing every vestige of self-control. Four days to reinforce her decision to keep things light between them. Four days to remind herself that it would just be a drink between friends, nothing more. Four days...

By the time Saturday rolled around, Chrissy had made those two words into a kind of mantra. And now there were no days left. She'd done the laundry, cleaned the flat, done the food shopping, made dinner for the next few days, and even managed to find time for a mani-pedi, but there were still two hours left before Rory would arrive to wreak havoc on her peace of mind. Hell, he wasn't around, but he was already doing a stellar job of it, anyway. She sighed as she stripped and stepped under the hot water of the shower. Her body ached with tension, and as she washed herself, she hoped the hot water would help relax her muscles.

It really was ridiculous how pent-up Rory made her feel. Stepping onto the plush bathmat, she dried herself slowly, eyeing her features as they became clearer in the slowly defogging mirror. Her heart-shaped face, with its high cheekbones and wide lips, were pleasant enough, and everyone commented on her pretty dimples. She loved the color of her skin the most ... it was a connection to the parents she had never known, a way for her to claim a heritage she barely understood.

Wrapping herself in the terry bathrobe behind the door, she headed over to the big old wardrobe in her bedroom and stood before its open doors, trying to decide what to wear. Casual, he'd said, but that only meant she didn't have to dress to the nines. Her small stature meant she would need to find something that would let her stand out next to the rockstar she'd be with, a man who could have his pick of any tall, willowy, gorgeous woman he chose, who she knew had runway models dying to be seen with him.

She was just an ordinary girl, short and round, with nothing to recommend her. Her job was nothing special … she was a glorified secretary. Nothing about her screamed "girlfriend to a star." And after she had shut down their burgeoning relationship, there was more than enough reason to suppose that that would never be her description. No woman looking at her with her straightened hair, short fingernails, and sensible, low-heeled pumps would think her a threat if they set their sights on Rory.

"Come on, Christina. This is no time to go down negative rabbit holes. You're not applying for a 'girlfriend to a star' position. You're just going out for drinks with one."

She berated herself as she pulled a pair of black jeans from the closet and a long-sleeved black t-shirt festooned with creamy yellow butterflies. The jeans were new, bought when she'd gone shopping with Toni and her friend Karen, and they'd promised her that they made her arse look good. And since it seemed that she needed a boost of confidence, she'd wear them and hope she only got the kind of attention she could handle, preferably only from Rory.

When had she become this uncool, this weak and boring person? Granted, she'd never been brash—her upbringing and temperament being what they were—but for some reason, she was feeling especially lacking in confidence, which did not bode well for her evening out with the sexiest, most attractive and distracting man she had ever met. She really needed to get out more. Maybe the next time the other administrative assistants went out for drinks, she'd go with them instead of shutting herself off from socializing. She needed friends, people she could hang out with, share her fears and frustrations with, and get advice from. She could almost hear her Aunt Zelda's voice in her ear:

"No man is an island, Christina. It is not a sin to enjoy the company of others, to seek them out for the sole purpose of reminding yourself that you are a human being with needs that others can help you to meet."

She smiled as she dressed, remembering how her worldly aunt had been the one to give her "the talk," ensuring that she understood not only the mechanics of things but also that there was nothing wrong with wanting to be physically intimate with another person, whoever that person turned out to be. Aunt Zelda had come to her religious calling later in life, after living fully and losing the lover of her heart to war. *She* understood, in ways her more sheltered sister—who had been a nun from the beginning—never would, how it could be between lovers, and what it felt like to be in love.

Maybe she needed to call her aunt to get some perspective on what her conflicted feelings about Rory meant.

"Or maybe you should figure this out on your own, Chrissy. You left home to be on your own because you wanted a chance to spread your wings, to learn how to be a grown woman without the shelter and protection of your aunts. Lots of women do it every day. Stop whining and get on with it!"

Sometimes it helped to speak the words aloud to herself. It stopped her from dissolving into a panic. Now, should she wear the shirt inside or outside? She pulled it over her hips and twisted and turned to see herself in the mirror. Hmm ... maybe inside would be better. Worn outside, she looked too much like her aunts when they pottered around on a Saturday doing chores at home. The last thing she needed tonight was to look like a middle-aged nun.

The clock said she had twenty-five minutes to wait. She did her makeup, trimming her eyebrows just so and applying a light foundation to even out her skin tone before dusting bronzer over her cheeks and adding a touch of eyeliner. Her lips were wide and full ... should she draw more attention to them with a pop of color, or should she leave them an understated neutral tone and lightly glossed?

Her cellphone rang and she reached for it, still trying to decide.

"This is Chrissy."

"This is Rory," he teased. "I'm almost there."

"I'll be ready when you get here."

Choosing to go the understated route, she finished her makeup, grabbed her wallet and keys, and put them, with her phone, into a little string purse just as the knocker sounded on her door. Taking a deep breath, then another for good measure, she hurried to the door, reciting the things she had already checked—the cats had water, their litter boxes were clean, the nightlight was on, and the radio was playing low. They'd be fine for the little while that she'd be out.

Rory took her breath away when she opened the door to him. His stunning blue eyes gleamed at her in the light from the motion-activated bulb above his head. He was also wearing jeans that clung to his long, muscular legs and a six-pack-hugging t-shirt in a complementary blue that left nothing to the imagination. His muscles had muscles, and yet he didn't look like a hulking beast. A leather vest and shiny black boots completed his ensemble, making him look like the rocker he was. She felt his gaze like a weight on her as she stepped out to meet him, turning to lock her door.

"Hi." Her greeting was breathy when she turned back to him.

His smile lit her up inside. "Hi yourself. Shall we?"

Extending an arm, he led her to a silver Mercedes Benz and helped her in, closing the door before going around to the driver's side.

"You look lovely, Chrissy," he told her as he strapped himself in and started the engine. "I hope you'll enjoy yourself tonight."

"I'm sure I will," she replied with false bravado, lying through her teeth.

She wasn't sure of anything except that seeing him again, being this close to him, inhaling the scent of his cologne and that other masculine aroma that seemed to permeate the car, had catapulted her right back to where they'd been when she'd run the first time ... in a world of trouble. Why had she thought six months apart would make a difference to the way she responded to him? He was even more potent now than he had been then, his skin tanned golden by his time on tour in the Caribbean.

She was grateful that he didn't make small talk. She was in no fit condition to even attempt matching wits with him. All her energies were focused on calming the gentle trembling in her limbs and the stuttering of her breath. Riordan, world-famous rockstar, lead singer of a world-famous band, was calmly driving her down a busy London street to God knew where for drinks. How was this her life right now? And how would she get herself back under control without ghosting him again? Because there had to be a better way than that.

CHAPTER 3

S ully's was crowded when Rory led Chrissy inside. The cute little restaurant and bar was never any less so, though, but he worried that his little kitten—the thought of the nickname he'd given her made him smile—would clam up when she got inside. Keeping a hand at her back both to encourage her to keep moving and to support her if she needed it, he led the way to the back, where his table was always ready for him, and seated her, watching to see how she was reacting.

"Wow! This is unusual."

Rory cocked his head at her. "What is?"

"No one hollered at you or paid you any mind at all. Do they not know who you are?" She looked around and then shook her head. "But clearly they do, since you've got a table."

"Everyone who comes here knows me," he explained. "But no one makes a big deal of it by mutual agreement. The owner is my friend and he's got everything under control."

Her wide, slightly almond-shaped eyes glanced around swiftly before coming to rest on his face, a tentative smile stretching her full lips. The need to kiss them rode him hard. He'd wanted desperately to kiss her when she'd opened her door to him earlier, but he had made himself a promise that he intended to keep. He would go at her pace this time, because he wanted there to be more between them than a cautious acceptance or platonic friendship.

Six months had been enough time for him to know that he had to try again with Chrissy, to find out if she was his person. He understood, even as he studied the drink menu they'd just been handed, that every decision he would make from now on would be with her in mind. That wasn't something he was prepared to share with her just yet, however. Instead, he looked over at her as she read the choices and asked, "What would you like to start with?"

Her eyes shot to his, startled by his wording. "To start with? Are we having a binge-drinking evening?"

When she relaxed, Chrissy was a hoot. Like now, that response made him chuckle because she'd asked the questions with the most earnest expression on her face, as though she meant every word to be taken seriously. He couldn't always tell when she was joking. Now would be one of those times.

"Perhaps not binge-drinking, exactly, but we may have a few drinks, with some finger foods to soak them up. I'm driving you home, so I'll be sure to keep my drinking to a minimum for safety. But you're free to try whatever you wish."

Sully's had a drink menu that was almost as extensive as the food one, with a number of specialty drinks that made it one of the city's premier drinking establishments. The owner was a trained chef who turned his interest in the art of mixed drinks into the bar's specialties.

Chrissy dropped her eyes back to the menu, and Rory waited, already knowing he would only have a couple of beers at most and ginger ale. He hoped Chrissy wouldn't take the safe route, the way she had done a lot when they'd been together before. There were a few cocktails on the list that he'd like her to try, but he reminded himself not to push when she looked up.

"The ginger martini sounds like something I might like."

"That's a good one. I can recommend their ginger pork potstickers if you want to keep the same flavor profile. We can order a shared plate, if you'd like that."

"That sounds fine. But what will *you* have to mix things up a bit?"

I'll have your lips, please, Kitten. "The portions are large, so let's start with just that and see if we want anything else after, okay?"

"Okay."

He watched her pull her gaze from his, hiding her feelings from him. The first order of business in his personal life was to get Chrissy to relax always and completely when she was with him. There could never be anything more between them if she was always guarded around him. Raising a hand to get the attention of a server, he mulled over ways to start. Hopefully, a cocktail or two would begin the process of loosening her up, but he knew keeping her in her cups was neither a healthy nor a long-term solution.

He needed to find out more than the little he knew about her from their short acquaintance. *No time like the present, Ro.*

"How's work these days?" A more innocuous question he couldn't imagine, and he hoped it would set her more at ease.

"It's actually been pretty busy this week," she began, clasping her hands together on the table. "Dr. James is in talks with some new prospects."

"Prospects?"

"Potential donors. We're constantly on the lookout for new money to fund our programs. And Dr. James and the board are looking at adding to the fundraising activities so we can open another satellite branch in Birmingham."

"That's exciting. Let me know when and how donations are being accepted."

Charitable giving had been part of the fabric of his life for as long as Rory had known himself. It was the one thing that he and his father still saw eye to eye on. It wouldn't be a problem helping Hope House meet its new goals, and he was more than happy to do so when he knew it would please the woman he was wooing.

Wooing ... that was really what this was all about, wasn't it? An old-fashioned courtship designed to win him the prize he hadn't known he wanted until it had been snatched away from him.

Although she didn't know it, Chrissy's exit from his life six months ago had shocked his system profoundly, leaving him reeling from more than just embarrassment and hurt at being so summarily rejected. It had been a reminder and a wake-up call, and he would not ignore them.

The drinks arrived, followed closely by the food, and they dug in. Rory watched as Chrissy took her first sip, loving the way her cheeks bloomed in a happy smile as a sigh escaped her lips.

"This is delicious!" Her delighted exclamation was filled with surprise, as though she hadn't expected it to be. "I could happily indulge in this for the rest of the evening."

Rory chuckled. "I'm glad you're enjoying it. If you'd like, I can recommend other cocktails that are surprisingly good for you to try, as well."

"We'll see," she replied noncommittally, spearing a couple of the potstickers and placing them on her plate.

He swallowed some of the pale ale he'd ordered, dragging his eyes away from her lips when she parted them to bite into one of the treats. He placed two on his own plate and stuffed one whole into his mouth, desperate to distract himself from the decadent sounds she was making as the flavors hit her tongue. It was indeed delicious, but what he wanted to be tasting at the moment was not a seasoned dumpling stuffed with savory meat. He wanted to taste those lips, to suckle the tongue that peeked out to lick off a drop of the sauce left behind from the other bite she'd dipped into it.

Swallowing his groan in another gulp of beer, he ate his second potsticker and helped himself to two more. He couldn't talk just yet. Words he had to keep to himself, for now, might spill out and frighten his little kitten away. He concentrated on the burst of flavors coating his tongue, washed it down with more beer, and hoped Chrissy would say something to ease the tension creeping into his spine.

She took another sip of her drink and looked around before speaking. "How did you find this place?"

"Ned found *me*, actually. He's the owner, and we've been friends since primary school. We lost touch after that—his dad was in the armed forces, and they moved around a lot for a while—and then about ten years ago, he came to one of my concerts and we reconnected. When he told me his plan to open this place, I persuaded him to let me be his silent partner."

"So you're a part owner of this?" She looked around again, as though she was trying to see any evidence of his ownership in the surroundings.

"I suppose technically I am, but not really. Ned has repaid me most of the seed money I put in but allows me to keep a ten percent interest. Which means I own nothing, really, though any decisions he makes, he does me the courtesy of letting me in on before he implements them."

"And you're okay with that?" Now her eyes pierced his, curiosity shining in them.

"Why wouldn't I be? The business is his." It really was that simple as far as he was concerned.

They finished the potstickers after that, and Rory looked at her encouragingly. "What would you like to try next?"

She picked up the menu that had been left next to her place setting and studied it again before asking,

"Have you ever had the espresso martini? Or the dirty banana cocktail?"

"I've had both. The martini is delicious if you enjoy coffee. The banana cocktail is delicious with ice cream or banana fritters."

She hesitated, clearly trying to decide what to order. "I'll try one each of those then. And I'll trust you to pick something to eat along with them."

I'll trust you ... said without hesitation, but still a far cry from where he wanted her to be. He would take this though, because any level of trust was better than none at all. He raised his hand again, and their server returned, taking their newest order which included one each of the cocktails she wanted to try and warm banana fritters served with a scoop of the house-made banana ice cream. While he waited, he drained his beer, and watched her sway to the house music wafting through the speakers in a tastefully low tone.

"Would you like to dance?"

He hadn't meant to ask that, but apparently, his tongue had joined his heart in a revolt against common sense. Ah, well ... it was too late now. He tried not to show any emotion when she shook her head, looking around again.

"Not right now."

Chrissy didn't need to say the words, but Rory knew what she was thinking. No one else was dancing, and she didn't want to become the center of anyone's attention. She was a genuinely shy woman, with a deeper edge of reserve that he imagined had a lot to do with how she had been raised. He would never willingly expose her in any way that would make her feel vulnerable. He swallowed his disappointment—when had he decided that he wanted to dance with her, anyway?—and contented himself with listening as she hummed to the new tune flowing from the speakers.

She could carry a tune well, he realized, when she began to sing along, apparently oblivious to the way his eyes couldn't tear themselves away from her. He hummed quietly along, harmonizing with her melody, hoping she wouldn't notice what he was doing, and loving the intimacy of their new connection. He didn't wonder why, he was just grateful that she had relaxed enough to share this much more of herself with him, even if she was doing so unwittingly.

The new order arrived, and she went for the coffee cocktail first, sipping it delicately. He watched her lick her top lip and bit his bottom one to hold in his groan.

"Wow!" Her eyes bulged. "That's a really strong coffee flavor." The expression on her face said that it was not what she had been expecting, and she was not a fan.

"You don't have to finish it if you don't like it, love." The endearment slid off his incautious tongue, and he decided he'd pretend he hadn't said it. "Here, taste my beer. Consider it a palate cleanser, if you will."

He went for the glass to pour it for her, but she shocked him by taking the bottle from his hand and putting it to her lips where he had only moments ago pressed his own. He closed his eyes against the vision of her sucking down his drink and the internal image of her sucking on the head of his cock. Said cock, which had been half hard all evening, shot to full attention in his tight jeans, and it was all he could do not to squirm in his chair. *Bollocks!* He absolutely could *not* let his mind wander.

When she returned his beer to him, he left it where she'd placed it, choosing to swallow a mouthful of her coffee drink instead. Once his body was back under control, he'd finish it. Thankfully, the rest of their order was delivered before the silence between them could become awkward. It occurred to him that they hadn't done much talking, but he didn't see that as a negative point. It was good that they could be together in silence without the need to fill it with useless words. Everything they *had* said had been needful, pleasant, and interesting.

"This is much better."

Rory watched her take a second, larger mouthful of the banana cocktail, swallow, and nod in satisfaction. So his little kitten had a sweet tooth, eh? Good to know. It was just one of many details about her that he had not learned when they'd been together before. She clearly didn't like strong coffee. Was she into chocolates? White milk or dark?

"Oh, I'm firmly in the milk chocolate camp."

Damn, he'd spoken aloud without realizing it. That wasn't good. He covered his momentary confusion with the first words to spring to his mind.

"So am I, for the most part. I'm a chocoholic, and I'm sure I've spent enough coin at Cadbury World to fund a small nation." She chuckled, and he smiled at her. "Have you ever been there?"

"No, I haven't."

"Are you free tomorrow? We could go then."

Would she shoot him down again? He was leaving on Monday and wouldn't be back for a month while his band went on a mini tour in the UK. Thirteen cities spread over twenty-eight days before they were back in London to prep for their North American tour. He'd be busy for the rest of the year and into the beginning of the new year, but he was prepared to adjust his schedule to include as much time as he could spend with the woman once again vocalizing her enjoyment of the food choices he'd made.

"These are fabulous! I wonder how they're made."

He wasn't surprised that she hadn't immediately answered his question. One thing he had learned about her was that she didn't make spur-of-the-moment decisions. She scooped up more of the fritter with some ice cream and wrapped her lips around the lot. Rory watched helplessly as she made love to the dessert, pausing once to sip a bit of the cocktail before returning to the last of the fritter she'd been served. If he wasn't careful, she'd catch him...

"Aren't you going to have yours?"

Busted! He saw her looking at his serving, and he grinned. "Want more?"

Her skin flushed, and he kicked himself. He hadn't meant to embarrass her. "How about if I share it with you? I know how good it is."

Without waiting for her to answer, he stuck his spoon into the fritter, cutting off a piece with a dollop of ice cream, and reached across the table.

"I'll have the rest, after you have this last bite."

He let her take the spoon from him and watched her pull the treat delicately off it with her teeth. If he could have, he would have done a fist pump in triumph because he understood at once what she was doing. Or rather *not* doing. She was making sure not to leave any trace of herself on the spoon aside from where her teeth made contact, because she wanted to avoid the intimacy inherent in them sharing the same spoon.

It was easy to act innocent and take his first mouthful without making a big deal of it, but he slid his tongue under the bottom of the spoon and moaned like a porn star, forcing her to glance at him while he sucked it clean.

"It really is delicious," he said, looking away so she wouldn't see the triumph in his eyes at the way her own widened and desire flashed in them before she turned away.

He finished his dessert in a couple more bites, giving her the reprieve that he knew she needed. Then, as he sipped from the water glass, he cycled back to his invitation.

"You didn't say whether or not you're free to go to Cadbury World with me tomorrow."

Sweets for the sweet, he thought, and what better place to continue this courting journey he'd started on than the place where the food of love was made? All she had to do was say yes.

"Didn't you say you were going back on tour soon? I don't want to make any extra work for you."

The tightness around her mouth was unacceptable. He knew that part of her problem with him was what might happen when he went on tour. She had not handled the fan reactions well, especially that first time when the groupie, who had been high as a kite, had bared her breasts at him. That didn't happen often, but there were no guarantees for a band, and he and his mates had learned to ignore the temptations that such fans represented. In that way, at least, they were not the stereotypical rock band.

"I leave on Monday, so tomorrow will be my last day off for a month. It would give me a great deal of pleasure if I could spend it with you. It's a two-and-a-half-hour drive up to Birmingham, and after the tour, we can have dinner before I bring you home. I promise you'll be back in time to get a proper night's rest before work on Monday."

Her hesitation was killing him, but he maintained a cool facade, finishing the glass of water and signaling for the server.

"Would you like anything else?" he asked her when the young man appeared at his side.

"No, thank you." A faint smile accompanied her answer.

"Then may I have the bill, please?"

CHAPTER 4

Chrissy waited until the server left before answering Rory's invitation. She didn't want to seem too eager, even if her initial reaction to his question had been a loud "yes" in her head. Against her better judgment, she had come out with him for drinks, and he'd been his usual charming self. But there had been a sharper edge to his charm, something more pressing that she was unable to ignore. How could she have walked away six months ago determined to forget the feelings he evoked, to forget him, because he stirred her up beyond what she felt able to manage, and yet now be beyond willing to go wherever he led?

The silence was awkward now, and it was her fault. *Just say yes, Chrissy!*

"I'd like that," she began, fumbling for words, then swallowed and added, "To go with you, that is."

Lord, what an idiot! He would probably see this time around that she was really not the woman he should be pursuing because she couldn't even answer a simple question without sounding like a fool. His smile distracted her from her self-deprecating inner tirade. It was wide and warm, and even she could see that her answer pleased him. Well, thank God for that! At least they'd end the night on a positive note. Maybe she could gain some cool in her sleep and make a better showing tomorrow. A girl could hope, right?

"I had a good time this evening," he told her as they walked up to her front door half an hour later. "I hope you did, too."

She turned before opening the door to smile at him, happy to be able to put his mind at ease about this one thing, at least.

"I did, thanks, Rory. Everything was lovely."

She wished in that moment that she could relax and let how she really felt flow from her lips instead of sounding like an uptight schoolmarm. *This right here is why you needed to move away from home.* It had been almost two years, and she was still channeling her staid Aunt Clare in her speech and mannerisms.

"Thanks for inviting me."

"It was my pleasure, love." His smile added another beam of light to the one that had flashed on as they approached the door. "Can you be ready by nine in the morning?"

"Yes, I can." She'd be up at the crack of dawn, knowing herself as well as she did. "Shall I pack a picnic?"

He paused, considering the idea. "You don't have to," he began, clearly reluctant, but she interrupted him.

"I want to contribute, please." She made her voice firm to indicate that she was serious and would brook no argument.

"Alright then," he relented. "Nothing too heavy, though, as we'll be having an early dinner."

Turning away, she unlocked her door and turned back to face him one last time. "I'll see you in the morning, then. Goodnight."

She hadn't intended to do more than that, but when he leaned in, she did as well and their lips touched. Lord help her, she had forgotten how his kisses burned her, how they set her skin alight with zinging sparks of electricity. She gasped, and he slipped his tongue in just enough for her to taste him. This shouldn't be happening. She eased back from his lips, though she couldn't stop herself from licking her own to chase the flavor of him left on them.

"Goodnight, little kitten," he whispered against her lips before stepping back and walking away to his car.

She watched him get in and start the engine, then returned his wave before going in and closing the door softly behind her. A quiet sigh escaped as she wandered into the kitchen to check on Pickles and Lynx. The cats were asleep, though they did each open an eye to observe her for a brief moment before returning to their slumber. Satisfied, she spent a few minutes looking at the contents of her cupboards and refrigerator and decided she'd make Scotch eggs, which meant putting the packet of frozen sausages in the refrigerator so it'd begin to thaw. Then she took herself off to bed. She'd shower in the morning. Right now, all she wanted to do was lie back and think of Rory. A chuckle escaped her at that thought as she curled onto her side.

They hadn't gone far enough in their relationship before for more than a few heavy make-out sessions. The one time they'd gone so far that she had thought ending up in his bed was inevitable, they'd been interrupted by his father's phone call. It had given her enough time to realize that she wasn't ready to be with someone whose life was constantly lived in the limelight. Even earlier tonight, in a place where he was safe from prying eyes, every time she had looked around, someone was watching them.

She had recognized more than one indulgent smile directed their way as they'd eaten, and though no one approached their table, it was clear after a while that everyone knew who he was. Was she any more prepared to be with him now than she'd been six months ago? Just because her whole body lit up whenever he was near didn't mean they were any better suited now than she'd thought they were then.

What would happen tomorrow in Birmingham? Cadbury World was a public place. The chances of him not being recognized were slim to none. Which reminded her ... what was she going to wear? How did one dress to spend a few hours in a chocolate factory? *Go to sleep, Chrissy. You'll need to be alert tomorrow.* She would worry about clothes when she woke up.

As usual, the cats had joined her in bed while she slept, one on either side of her so that they were a kind of fur-and-flesh sandwich. Reaching for her cellphone, she yawned widely and straightened the sleep bonnet covering her hair before she took a picture. She'd send it to her aunts later. They hadn't seen her in a while, and she knew they worried about her. This would show them that she was fine. Her feline protectors had her back ... and her front. Laughing softly at her silly thoughts, she set the phone down and scooped an arm around each beast.

"I'm sorry, boys, but I must eject you from my bed. I have places to go and chocolate to buy." The cats mewled plaintively, and she glanced at the clock on her side table. "Alright. Let's get you some food."

Once they'd been fed, she set about preparing the snacks for the day's outing, munching on toast and marmalade as she worked. The Scotch eggs were the most time-consuming to make, but while the eggs boiled, she cored and sliced two apples, placing them in two plastic baggies on the kitchen island, added nut butter and a butter knife, as well as two scones, cream, and jam. Then she pulled the sausages from the refrigerator, zapped them in the microwave for thirty seconds, and seasoned them.

Once all the steps had been taken and her sausage-covered eggs were simmering in the hot oil, she fetched the picnic basket and packed in the rest of the food. Brewing a quick cuppa, she sipped it while she completed the picnic prep. Aside from water, the only beverage she had, if she didn't take tea or coffee with her, was the bottle of wine that Karen had handed to her at Toni's reception when they were cleaning up, before she and Niall left for their honeymoon. It would have to do, since she had no idea what would go best with the food she had prepared. She only knew she wanted to impress Rory, who was, after all, the son of a nobleman as well as a wealthy man in his own right.

By the time the food was all ready and the Scotch eggs in their insulated container, it was eight o'clock and she had yet to pick out an outfit. *No need to rush, girl, you've still got an hour.* She still bustled back into her bedroom and flung the wardrobe door open, peering in at the few summer dresses she owned. Perhaps the yellow one? It was a mid-calf-length Boho-style garment with puff sleeves, a high waist, and a slit to mid-thigh on her left leg.

With no time left to hem and haw over whether or not she really wanted to show so much leg—and she knew her Aunt Clare would be appalled at the "excessive" display—she took a hurried shower and quickly dressed, spritzing herself with some of her favorite scent. Checking one last time to make sure that her minimal application of makeup was sufficient, she was just stepping back into the kitchen when the knocker sounded.

"Coming!" She opened the door and lost her breath.

Rory looked scrumptious in a color-block stand-collar shirt in black and burgundy, white shorts, and black canvas slip-ons on his sock-less feet. The short, rolled sleeves of his shirt emphasized his heavily defined biceps, and the two buttons left undone at his throat brought the strong column of his neck into sharp relief. She inhaled and caught a whiff of his cologne and did her best not to swoon at the picture he made.

"Hi! The picnic basket is in the kitchen," she said, stepping aside so he could pass her into the hallway.

"I had an idea as I was coming over," he told her, following her into the kitchen. "We won't get there till almost lunchtime, so what if we have our picnic first and then take in the sights?"

"That's fine. I just wonder, would you prefer to take this bottle of wine, or do you want to stop and get soft drinks?"

"Why don't we save the wine for another time? I don't mind water," he gestured to the bottles she had packed. "And if you can, maybe a flask of tea?"

"I can do that. It'll be a little longer."

She turned to put the wine back into the refrigerator when he caught her around the waist and spun her back to face him.

"Hi!"

He leaned in and captured her lips in a sweet hello, then let her loose and stepped back behind the kitchen island. How she managed to steady herself enough to finish brewing the tea, she couldn't say, but eventually, everything was packed into the basket, and Rory was leading the way back out to his car. Once they were on their way, he glanced over at her with a smile.

"You look great, love."

He glanced down at her lap before turning his attention back to the road, much to her relief. She was too wound up and needed just a little more time to reset her internal controls.

"We'll have our picnic lunch in Bournville Park before heading to Cadbury World. You said you've never been there, right?"

Thankful for the change of subject, Chrissy shook her head. "I haven't been to too many places, really. Before I moved to London, I lived all my life in Ely with my aunts. They rarely went anywhere, except once or twice to the seaside. I went with them, of course, and I also once went to Rhyl in Wales on a school trip. But I was never much of a social butterfly."

"What did you do for entertainment if you spent most of your time at home?"

There was no trace of pity or mockery in his voice, and that pleased her, helping her to relax even more. She might not be especially worldly, but she would have nothing to do with anyone's pity. She'd lived a happy life, grateful for the blessings she had received when her aunts had told her the story of her life at age ten. She'd been curious about why she lived with two nuns and had asked where her mother and father were.

Knowing she'd been abandoned at birth had been bittersweet, but she had practiced thankfulness because she knew that there were other children in her school who lived with foster parents, whose demeanor told the story of their private misery. Her aunts had adopted her, and she belonged with them, with their family, in a way those children never would. The thought made her smile even as she answered his question.

"I read a lot, played solitaire, and for a while in my teens, I wrote poetry. And there were hikes and bike rides, and visits to fun fairs." She paused, realizing as she said the next words that they were true even though she hadn't consciously been aware of that fact. "I was never very interested in going anywhere or doing anything special. I liked being alone far more than I liked being in company."

"Did you have boyfriends?"

"No. I was too quiet for any boy to notice me, really. I had girlfriends, and we sometimes would go to the cinema together, or to the ice cream shop. Some of them had boyfriends. That was as close as I got to being around boys socially."

"What, you didn't even try? Not even at uni?" He sounded incredulous.

"I went to a vocational training college, and aside from the one boy who kept trying to get into my knickers..."

Rory interrupted her, his tone stiff. "How do you know that that was what he wanted?"

What was with his tone? Was he judging her somehow? Did he think she was too uptight?

"He told me so," she replied defensively. "Every time he asked me out, his invitation always included a mention of the fun we could have after whatever outing he suggested. I wasn't stupid enough to think he would wait until we knew each other well enough to sleep together." She shuddered as she remembered how things had escalated until she had had to report him to the college. "He tried to force me..."

This time Rory's interruption was clearly outraged. "What? I hope you reported his arse to the school."

"I did. I was lucky that one of my classmates happened along just as he tried strong-arming me back into my room."

"How did he know where you lived?"

She could hear the fury building in his voice, and she desperately wanted to diffuse the situation. She didn't need him driving while impaired by anger at something that had happened in her past.

"He walked me home the first time he asked me out. I didn't think anything of it then ... why would I?"

"Did he hurt you?"

Chrissy smiled. "Not physically, no, aside from the bruises where he'd held my arms. But it messed me up emotionally, as you can imagine. I had never been an outgoing person to begin with, and that just pushed me over the edge."

The silence that followed her words was not uncomfortable, though she did wonder what he was thinking and what he would ask her next. She hadn't thought about that experience for years, and now it no longer had the power to make her shudder in fear.

"And yet, you came to London on your own to live alone. You may not be outgoing, as you say, but you're very brave."

Admiration laced his words this time. *Was* she brave, as he thought? Perhaps, but she didn't see it in those terms. For her, it was just another step in the maturing process. Her aunts were older women who wouldn't be with her forever, and it behooved her to ensure that she could stand on her own two feet before they passed. She had no one in the world aside from them. It was in the interest of self-preservation that she had made the move.

"I don't know about that. I just needed to grow up, to be sure I could handle being an adult without the supervision of two people who could pass on at any moment. I needed to learn to be independent."

He reached over briefly and squeezed her hands, where they lay loosely in her lap.

"You're doing a pretty good job of it, then."

Except when it comes to relationships. She was still missing out in the boyfriend department.

"You just need a bit more practice there. And I'm happy to be your guinea pig."

"What?" She turned to look at him, her brow furrowed in confusion. What was he on about?

"You said you're not managing so well with relationships." He glanced at her, one brow quirked questioningly.

Good Lord! She hadn't meant to say that aloud. Shaking her head slightly, she hastened to answer him.

"I wouldn't want you to feel obligated," she said lamely. She wasn't trying to reject him again, but it was embarrassing to be having this conversation with the man she had ignored for six months after they'd been building a friendship.

"Do I sound like that's how I feel?" A hint of impatience colored his tone this time.

"No, you don't." *Stop talking, Chrissy. Quit while you're ahead.*

He didn't respond to that, leaving her to wonder if she had offended him. If he needed any further proof that she was bad at relationships, she'd just handed it to him. Silence seemed golden right now. It wasn't as though there was anything she could say to make the situation any less awkward, was there?

"We'll have to work on trust between us, won't we?"

Startled, Chrissy looked over at the man whose whole attention seemed to be on the road ahead of them.

"It's not that..."

He interrupted her again. "It is, love. You just haven't recognized it as yet."

He paused, opened his mouth as if to say something more, then closed it without speaking. She considered his comment. He was probably right. After James, she had closed herself off to every man who even looked at her with interest, making sure they understood that she wasn't interested.

"I know you've probably figured this out already, but I need to say it anyway. For my peace of mind. There are a lot of men who are twats, who don't deserve your trust, and you are right to be cautious with them. But there are many who are gentlemen, who will protect you and wait for your consent, who will respect and honor you. You should give *them* a chance."

What he *didn't* say, what was left hanging in the air between them, understood if unvoiced, was that *he* was one of those gentlemen, and she should give *him* a chance. And she would.

CHAPTER 5

One conversation, and Rory understood more about Chrissy than he had in all the time they'd been together before. Clearly, they hadn't talked enough back then, a situation he planned to remedy. He hated that she'd been pushed back into her shell by one arsehole of a man who thought he could take a woman's consent as his right, whether he actually received it or not. He shuddered to think what could have happened if her friend hadn't intercepted him. Chrissy might be a broken woman today.

The thought made his chest ache. She was a sweet and uncomplicated woman who didn't ask for anything from anyone, but who pulled every protective instinct that he had buried inside him to the surface. He would work on building her trust in him, so that when he finally told her all that he wanted with her, she would be receptive to it.

"Do you mind if I queue some music?" He needed to ease the subtle tension that had built up in the car as they'd talked.

"No, I don't mind." She avoided looking at him, a sure sign that the conversation had distressed her.

He had a set of playlists ready for when he did long drives or road trips, and he settled on the third one, which was a compilation of Third Generation's earlier work. The songs were full of optimism and light, just the mood he wanted to establish. The first, an original that he'd written long before he and the others got together, broke into the silence with a tremendous crash of sound. He let the words flow over him, hoping they would soothe his little kitten as they did him.

"One hundred years, forever, and a day,
You've filled my hungry heart and made it beat.
You are its rhythm true, its melody.
A hundred years are not enough, my sweet."

He remembered writing that song. Funny that people imagined it was because he was in love. Truth be told, it had been his parents' wedding anniversary—their twenty-second, if memory served—and he'd come in on them kissing in the kitchen. They hadn't noticed him at first, and he'd had just enough time to wonder what two over-forty adults were thinking, acting like teenagers where anyone could see them, when his dad had lifted his head. The look on his face as he whispered something in his mother's ear had made a sharp pang of longing pierce Rory's chest.

Then they'd noticed him and turned to look at him, their arms still around each other as his mother said, "Do you need something, Rory?"

"No ... no. I'm fine. Sorry to interrupt."

He'd turned away then, wishing the ground would open up and swallow him, but before he was out of earshot, he heard his father's words. "It feels like yesterday, doesn't it, my darling? You're the beats of my heart, forever and a day."

Who knew his father was so poetic and romantic? The words sounded like lyrics ... maybe he could play around with them and compose a song. He was taking a poetry class, so he'd had fodder for his imagination, and before too much longer, "Forever And A Day" was born.

"Did you write this song?"

Chrissy's question snapped him out of his thoughts. "Yes. I write most of the original material that we sing. Why?"

He could feel her gaze on his profile as she said, "Well, it's a love song, isn't it? You don't write lyrics like those without being in love."

Rory kept the smile off his face at her studiedly neutral tone. What was she thinking? Was she jealous, imagining him loving some other woman? He'd thought he had, for a while back when ... he cut the thought short. Not now, certainly not with the woman he was sure he had fallen for months earlier.

"Actually, my parents inspired that song," he told her. He couldn't allow her to think he had an interest in anyone but her. "They've been married now for over forty years, and you'd think they were half their age the way they carry on sometimes."

His relationship with his father may have become strained over the last decade and a half, but Rory still admired him for the obvious love he showed his wife. That, more than anything else, had been part of the reason that he had never felt comfortable with hookups. It was why he'd begun to search for his own heartbeat, why he thought he'd found it again in Chrissy, why he was finally considering a compromise that would ease the tension between him and his dad and win him the woman of his dreams.

Her sigh was weighted longing. He remembered her story and understood that perhaps even his poor relationship with his dad was better than never knowing him at all. He held his peace, not wanting to add to whatever weight she was carrying. This was meant to be a happy day of fun and camaraderie. There had been quite enough of the heavy conversations. He was ready to move on to the fun part of the day.

By the time they got to the park, thankfully without incident, the sun was pelting down, the chill of the morning dispelled beneath its rays. They found a pleasant spot under a tree near the stream and settled down to enjoy their lunch. The stream babbled along next to them, and a few people strolled by, all enjoying the quiet serenity of the park.

"It's really pretty here."

Chrissy looked around her while Rory stared at her lips as she ate. After the next bite of her scone, a crumb remained on her lower lip, and

Rory watched as it hung precariously before she became aware of it and licked it off. He looked away just as she turned to him, and bit into the Scotch egg he'd been holding for the last minute.

"Mmm, this is delicious!" He took another bite, savoring the blend of flavors. "You did well."

"Thank you. Would you like some tea with that?"

"Don't mind if I do."

"Honey, milk, sugar?"

"Just honey, please ... two teaspoons."

He took the travel mug that she handed him and sipped. "Perfect. Maybe when we go in, we can have an ice cream?"

"If there's room, sure." Her smile was warm as she patted her belly.

Laughter floated by them as a family walked past, the father pushing a double pram while the mother wrangled a toddler who was running ahead and laughing joyously as he played catch with her. Would he ever have children? Did Chrissy want them? How long before she wasn't able to bear young any longer? Neither of those was a question he thought was appropriate to ask so soon into their renewed relationship, but he *would* ask, someday.

"I haven't been out like this in a while."

He glanced over at her, but she was gazing into the burbling water. "Why not?"

She looked down at her hands, then picked up one of the eggs and studied it as though the answer to his question was hidden in it. Then she shrugged.

"I dunno. Probably because I didn't have anyone to share the day with. The few people I wouldn't mind doing that with all have fulfilling lives with people with whom they would much rather spend their time."

He noticed the complete lack of self-pity in her tone. She was merely stating the facts as she knew them. He wanted to hold her so hard, to tell her that he would always be there when she needed a companion, that when she was ready, he would be more if she'd let him. Instead, he nodded his agreement.

"Picnicking alone is a bore, I agree. Not to mention that it might make you look a little bit pitiful. And you don't seem like the type to want that kind of negative attention."

She chuckled ruefully. "You'd be right about that." She wiped her mouth and fingers on a napkin and began to clean up.

Lunch over, they stowed the picnic things and drove the two minutes to Cadbury World, and for the next few hours, they strolled through the various parts, listening to the guide provide information about the history of the candy, the ingredients, how they're blended together, and everything related to the bars. They stood by one of the windows and watched as the chocolate makers carved a fastidious old-fashioned lady's boot.

"That's so incredible," Chrissy gushed. "I have such great respect for people who can do work like this."

They did the exhibition tour, the 4D African Adventure, rode the little train through the grotto, played with chocolate in the hands-on section, and ended up in "The World's BIGGEST Cadbury Shop" so Chrissy could fill her chocolate needs "for the rest of the year," as she said. Rory persuaded her to pose in front of the building with the cartoon characters working that day, as well as next to the life-sized, purple-and-white cow in the cafe, and in front of the car on the green decorated with images of different chocolate treats. When they headed back to his car, she was carrying a large purple Cadbury tote bag filled with her favorite chocolate treats as well as a couple of souvenir mugs.

"I hate that the Americans have taken over our chocolate company," she said as she settled into her seat, strapping herself in. "Why do they have to control everything? Why couldn't this institution have remained ours?"

She sounded quite miffed, and he supposed he could understand that. She wasn't alone in her dislike of the hostile takeover, and he didn't try to make her feel better. What was the use? Something quintessentially British had been strong-armed into submission by their big, bad neighbor across the pond because money talked in the modern world, whether they liked it or not. He distracted her, instead, by asking her when she found out that she was a chocoholic. Her amused giggles were music to his ears.

"My Aunt Zelda, who is the younger of the two sisters, told me the first time I had a piece I was a baby, and she was trying to get me to stop crying. I must have been about a year old or so, she said, and I was teething or something. Anyway, she slipped me a bit of the bar she was enjoying—because Aunt Clare, the older one, would not have allowed it if she knew—and I quieted right down."

She laughed as the memory took hold. He loved the sound. It was warm and musical. He could write songs about it. Shaking his head at his fanciful thought, he refocused on her as she kept talking.

"After that, she couldn't have chocolate without sharing it with me, apparently. So the short answer is that I've loved chocolate all my life."

"What's your favorite bar?"

"Dairy Milk, without question." She turned to him, curiosity lacing her voice as she asked, "What about you? What's *your* favorite bar?"

"I love the Whole Nut. I have a thing for nuts."

He did his best not to chuckle at the naughty thought that followed his words. It seemed that being with Chrissy brought out the randy in him, which wasn't a problem, as long as she didn't realize it. He didn't want her thinking his only interest in her was sexual.

"That's my second favorite. I love hazelnuts."

Silence descended between them, but he didn't mind it. He queued another playlist and they enjoyed soothing instrumentals. When they were almost back in London, he asked the question he'd been keeping close to the vest all day. Would she be amenable to the idea?

"How would you like to have dinner at my place? We can order in, or I can make you something simple."

"You cook, too?"

She tried valiantly to hide her shock, but he heard it and it made him chuckle. "Do I seem that helpless to you?" he asked.

"No. It's just..." She trailed off.

What could she possibly have thought to make her so surprised? "It's just ... what?" he had to know.

"Well, I thought..." She paused, clearly choosing her words. "I mean, a man like you..."

She stopped speaking again, apparently unable to find a way to say whatever was on her mind. Did she think he would be offended? He didn't care.

"Just tell me. And then I'll prove to you that I am a man of many talents."

He turned to head in the direction of his home and let her compose her response. They had all the time in the world, and he hoped she wouldn't notice how he'd taken the decision about dinner out of her hands. Either way, he'd have her in his personal space for the first time since they'd met. He couldn't wait to see how she would react.

"Please don't be offended," she began again. "But I just never imagined that a man like you, with more money than he knows what to do with, would be bothered to learn to cook when you can just hire someone to do it for you."

"My hands are good for more than playing guitar and piano, love," he replied, laughing at her words and being deliberately suggestive.

Let her make of that what she would. He would do his damnedest to get to where he could show her *all* the things he could do with his hands, not just *for* her, but *on* her and *in* her. His body lit up at that thought, and he eased his arse on the seat in an effort to lessen the tension gathering in his crotch. He absolutely refused to get any harder than he'd been all day.

His house was in one of London's wealthy suburbs, and his privacy was ensured by the high walls surrounding it, the large, heavy metal gates keeping unwanted visitors out, and the hidden gem of a landscaped and terraced backyard complete with a swimming pool, hot tub, and an outdoor living room and kitchen. He parked the car in front of the house, since he had to take her back to her flat after dinner and led her inside.

"Welcome to my home, Chrissy."

He walked away from where she stood just inside the front door and let her take in the high ceiling and grand staircase. He had had the house extensively renovated on the inside, though no one approaching would know that from the outside. He liked elegant simplicity, and the six-bedroom mansion he'd bought for a song allowed him to marry those two concepts beautifully.

"This entryway is impressive," she told him, eyes still directed up to the crystal chandelier.

"I did a lot of gutting and refitting in the house," he answered, "because it was a little too narrow and drafty for my liking. But I liked the bones of the place, and most of it is the same as it was before. I'm pleased that you like it."

She looked down to catch his eye. "How many bedrooms?"

He held her gaze for a long moment before replying, "Six."

"Oh! That's ... quite a few."

He could tell there was more on her mind, but she withheld it and he didn't press. They could revisit all the things she wanted to say but held back another time, when they had established a closer bond.

"Come through," he said, leading the way into the kitchen.

"I see what you mean about refitting. You've included all the mod cons in here, haven't you?"

"When I'm here, I like to be as comfortable as I can be, because I'm so often on the road without the comforts of home."

"I can understand that."

"I'll give you the tour in a few, I just need to get some things out in preparation for dinner."

He pulled the leftover beef Bolognese from the freezer and a packet of fresh tagliatelle noodles to go with it. He'd make Caesar salad for them to share when he got back down. Maybe she would help him. Cooking together was another way to build a connection not based on sex, and he was all for it.

"Come on, then," he invited her. "Let's do the penny tour."

He led her back into the front hall and up the stairs to the second floor, where four of the bedrooms, a sitting room, and two Jack-and-Jill bathrooms occupied the space.

"When the lads and I have a late night in the studio downstairs, or they're here for a party, they often crash up here. That's part of why I bought such a big house. It's nice to have company sometimes."

He had kept the color scheme simple, blue and white throughout, with heavy velvet drapes at the windows. The floors were a dark wood, elegant, and easy to clean. Area rugs throughout kept feet from getting too cold in the winter.

"I'm up here," he told her, pointing up the narrower staircase to the third floor. He let her go ahead of him, studiously keeping his eyes off her round, delectable bottom, and when they were both standing in the bedroom at the foot of his bed, he said, "There used to be two bedrooms up here, but I had them re-organize the space so I could have a full bathroom and an office as well as a larger master."

She grinned impishly at that. "I see ... no hob-nobbing with the plebs, or unintentional sharing of embarrassing fart noises, huh?"

He laughed, shocked at her words, but still delighted that she had relaxed with him enough to make such an explicit joke. "Something like that. Despite my job, I'm a pretty private man. I prefer to keep my bodily functions to myself, thank you very much."

She laughed with him for a second until whatever new thought popped into her mind wiped the smile from her face and replaced humor with unease. Her moods were so mercurial, borne along on the whims of her thoughts and feelings.

"What?" When she looked away without speaking, he went to where she stood and took her hand. "Tell me. There's nothing you can ask or say that will upset me, love."

She tried to pull her hand away, but he resisted, keeping hold of it and using his other hand to raise her chin so her eyes met his.

"Tell me."

"It doesn't matter. It was a really rather impertinent and inappropriate thought," she said, snapping her lips shut again.

"More inappropriate than a fart joke?" His voice held a sharper edge than he intended it to have.

When he saw the chagrin on her face at the reminder that she had, in fact, said something off-color, he sighed. There were minefields everywhere with her, and he'd just have to roll with the punches and defuse every mine he stumbled upon without letting either of them get hurt.

"Just tell me, Chrissy. Your joke was funny, so don't even go there."

She swallowed and complied. "Well, again, you're an eligible bachelor, you're very attractive, and you must have had a ... companion or two here. I just wondered if at any of those parties, when the band members were all together, you were glad your bedroom was on a different floor so no one would hear ... *those* sounds."

Her cheeks flushed darkly with mortification. Poor baby! He hurried to reassure her both about the activities he engaged in here and about her having thought about them.

"You're the only woman, aside from my mum and my little sister, who has set foot in this bedroom."

Rory let that sink in, watching as the color in her cheeks deepened even more. If nothing else, at least knowing that she was the only woman who'd been given a tour of his bedroom would show Chrissy that of all the women she thought he had had in his life before her, she was special. Then, before she could speak—because she might not even believe him, given his job and his dating history—he elaborated.

"I would never disrespect the woman I was with by making noisy love to her with anyone else in the house. This is my private haven, and I only open it to the lads for sleepovers once in a while."

He let her go then and stepped over to the large bay window overlooking his backyard oasis. He beckoned to her, and when she came over to where he stood, he said, "I like sitting here of a morning with my tablet and a cuppa, enjoying the peaceful scene, letting my mind wander."

He sat on the plush purple cushioning and pulled her down to sit next to him. She closed her eyes and he smiled. The seat was comfortable, and he had dozed off a time or two while sitting here daydreaming.

"Comfy, isn't it?"

She nodded but didn't speak, so he went on when she opened her eyes. "That door," he pointed to his left, "leads to the bathroom. I'll show you when we're ready to leave. That one," he indicated the open one on their right, "is my closet. And the little office I mentioned is accessed through a door in the back of the closet where the shoe rack is. It actually hangs over the door so it moves when I open it."

"It's not very full, is it?"

"Judging me by everyone else's standards again, love?" he teased, relieved when she didn't react. "I've just had a clear-out, which is something I do after every extended tour. Besides, a man can only wear one outfit at a time, right? What's the point of having too many?"

"That's very minimalist of you." There was no sarcasm. Just another observation.

"You know what they say ... less is more, yeah?"

She eased a smile back onto her face. "That's true. I guess that means you don't get attached to things like the rest of us do."

"Well, not to clothes, no. But I do have a favorite guitar, and I have kept other paraphernalia related to the band and my writing."

She stood up and walked toward the closet. "May I see your office before we go back down?"

So she was ready to leave. Being in his bedroom wasn't putting her more at ease. No problem ... they would cross that bridge when they got to it. He led her obligingly through the door into his office, which held an ancient mahogany desk, littered with sheet music and other papers, an ergonomic office chair, a tall, thin bookshelf filled to overflowing with some of his favorite reading material, and a deep, comfy chair bestrewn with cushions and a blanket.

"Is that your favorite guitar?" She pointed to the box guitar on the wall across from his desk.

"It is. My dad gave it to me when I was eleven. It was brand new then, of course."

She walked over and drew a finger over the wood, lingering on each scratch as though she wanted to caress away the instrument's pain. She was going to kill him with these unintended and wholly innocent yet erotic actions. Clearing his throat, he said, "Why don't I show you the bathroom, and then we'll go down for the rest of the tour, hmm?"

She exclaimed delightedly over the black-and-white coloring in his bathroom, declared that his shower and tub could easily accommodate Jesus and the twelve apostles—which made him laugh uproariously—and asked permission to touch his towels because, "I've been trying to find new bath towels, but everything I've seen so far is too coarse."

"Help yourself," he managed to say before turning his eyes away so he wouldn't have to watch her making love to the towels he used to wash and dry his skin. Those hands should be smoothing *him* down, not his towels!

"These actually feel quite good. Where did you buy them?"

"I didn't. My mum got them for me. I'll ask..."

"No, please, don't bother. I'll just remember the brand and search for them online."

She stepped out then, and they went back downstairs where he showed her the larger formal drawing room and smaller lounge with the wide screen television and the stereo system, the bedroom with ensuite bathroom where his parents could stay so they didn't have to climb the stairs, the kitchen and rather small—by comparison—dining room.

"I took some square footage off the dining room to enlarge the living quarters for my parents. And anyway, I don't eat in here if I can avoid it," he told her. "The kitchen table is large enough for me."

"You said something about a studio when we were upstairs. Where's that?"

"Down this way."

He turned and walked to the door that led down a set of steps to the walkout lower level of the house that opened onto a terraced landscape. The water in the pool glistened in the late afternoon sunlight, which cast shadows from the trees over the covered hot tub and over the lawn and flower beds.

"Maybe another day you can come over early enough to take a swim. The water is temperature controlled."

He threw out the invitation casually but didn't linger on it. She wanted to see his studio, so he turned and opened the door leading into the space that took up most of the lower level of the house.

"This is where the work happens," he said. "It's soundproofed and has special accommodations for the drums."

"I'm sure the neighbors appreciate the sound-proofing, even if they don't realize they do." She smirked as she said that, making him laugh.

"If you're interested, the next time we're working here, I can have you over to watch."

Another casual mention of something they could do together, another way to share his life with her. The more time he could spend with her, the greater his chance of breaking down her walls and getting to the heart of her. That was his goal.

"This is impressive."

She had moved past him to the recording and mixing equipment and was looking around her at all the other paraphernalia needed in the studio. Then her eyes caught on the guitars on the wall.

"Are these all yours?"

Rory nodded. "Yes. I use different ones depending on my mood or the song."

"Have you used the guitar upstairs recently? I mean, recorded a song with it?"

"I have a couple of songs on our latest album where I play it and there are no other instruments, yes. Why do you ask?"

"Well, these all seem new and flashy, but I rather like the one upstairs. It has a history and longevity. I think both those things are priceless, don't you?"

"Yes, they are. And sometimes, simplicity is all you need."

She walked back over to him and looked into his eyes. "I think I would very much like to watch you rehearse or record down here someday. Maybe the same day I come to test the warmth of the water in your pool."

She was smiling as she said that, and he returned it as broadly, beyond grateful that she had accepted both his invitations.

"When we get back in a month's time, I'll set it up. We have some new material to run through and will be working on a studio album before we go to North America. There'll be lots of time to bring you back then."

Back upstairs in the kitchen, he began the food prep, pleased when she offered to make the salad for him. The feeling of rightness that enveloped him as they worked together settled his resolve to make her his. Unless she didn't feel the same way that he did, in which case he'd have to live with her decision. That thought unsettled him ... he was putting all his eggs in one basket, as his mother constantly warned him against doing. How would he go on if she refused him in the end?

"Rory?"

He blinked. He had completely zoned out and gone to that negative place in his head where nothing went right. Snapping himself out of it, he apologized and asked her to repeat herself.

"I just asked if you have balsamic vinegar."

"Oh, yes. On the second shelf in that cupboard there."

Soon enough, the pasta was ready, and he added it to the Bolognese sauce, which was how he liked it. Letting them sit together for a few extra minutes, he turned his attention to drinks. He already knew that while she had the odd glass of wine on occasion, she wasn't especially a wine drinker. He'd have red wine with his dinner, but he needed to know what she would like to drink so he could set her up before they sat down to eat.

"Do you like sparkling water?"

"Depends. What flavor?"

He walked over to his drink cupboard and looked in. "I have plain and cherry Perrier."

"Cherry sounds good."

Finally, they sat at the kitchen table and dug in. The beef Bolognese was even better than it had been before, and Chrissy's moans of pleasure were gratifying. He chose not to interrupt their meal with conversation, preferring to watch her enjoy her food and listen to the evening sounds coming through the open window. Thank God she didn't feel the need to fill the silence with words that meant nothing. He was glad she didn't mind silence when there was nothing to say.

"Wow! Thanks for dinner, Rory. That was really good."

"You're welcome. I'm glad you enjoyed it."

She stood up and began to clear away the dishes. Rory didn't want her to do any cleaning up. He stood as well and took the dishes from her.

"You're my guest. I can't have you working for your supper."

"But..."

"Ah, ah, ah! No 'buts.' Maybe next time. Sit yourself down and wait for me."

She pursed her lips, not at all pleased that he wouldn't let her help, but he just smirked and cleared the table, loading the dishwasher for a change. The time he spent handwashing the few dishes they'd used—which was what he normally preferred to do—would be better spent with her.

"Would you like some dessert?" he asked, after he had wiped down the counter.

"No, thank you, I'm full."

He could almost see her brain ticking over, and he wondered what she was thinking. It was still early enough that they could hang out together for a bit longer.

"Then let's go and visit for a while longer in the lounge. Want anything else to drink, or perhaps a cup of coffee?"

"I'm fine, Rory, thank you."

Leading the way into the lounge, he picked up the remote control. "Which do you want to do ... watch something on the telly or listen to music?"

"What do *you* like to watch?"

"I mostly watch documentaries and nature programs, but I also love police procedurals and spy movies."

"We're so different. I'll watch those if there's nothing else on offer that I like, but I much prefer to watch sci-fi and fantasy and romances. They're my guilty pleasure."

"Why guilty?" He had sat beside her when she chose the love seat, and their knees touched when he leaned in.

"Well, it's all fiction, isn't it? Speculative, imaginative, *not* real. My aunts always caution me to beware of what I feed my soul. But I use it to escape from the real world."

"And what do you need to escape from?" he asked as he hit the start button to get a playlist of soft rock going.

"These days, mostly my thoughts."

It sounded like a confession she didn't seem happy to be making, but Rory held his peace, hoping that she would elaborate. She glanced up at him before continuing.

"Everyone has a purpose in life, something or someone that they're passionate about. I have nothing and no one. It's kind of a sobering thought, you know? Here I am past thirty and still with no real purpose."

"Everyone figures out their purpose in their own time. You know that. I would never judge you for being who you are. As long as you enjoy the things you do, the rest is icing on the cake."

"Don't you want to have someone who is your person? Someone to be passionate about?"

Ah, that was the crux of the matter, wasn't it? The reason for her disquiet. This was the perfect opportunity for him to be as honest and open as he knew how.

"I do, love. I have wanted it for more years than I realized, and then I met you. So it's been a while since I've consciously known that that's what I want." She held his gaze as realization dawned. But before she could respond, he continued, "We need to talk about what happened six months ago, about why you ran away and left me hanging. But

I think, until we can have that conversation, we should begin again to build trust, because I want more with you than a few dates and some kisses. I want to share my passion with you, if you'll let me."

"Why can't we talk now?"

"Because I promised to get you home in time to get good sleep for work, and because our flight leaves at seven-thirty in the morning. And even though it's only an hour-and-fifteen-minute flight, we need to get set up and do a bit of rehearsing, plus some PR stuff, before our first show tomorrow night. The crew is already on their way up in the buses."

He moved then, reaching out to pull her into his arms. She was warm and soft, and he wanted nothing more than to take the next step, but she might not be ready for that, and he was determined not to rush her this time. So he just held her, and when she relaxed and slumped against his side, he rested his chin on top of her head with a smile.

"This is nice."

Her soft admission, shyly spoken, was enough to make him release her so he could look into her eyes before he pulled her back in. "It is. And I'm free for cuddling whenever you need me, okay?"

She chuckled. "Be careful what you wish for," she warned him. "You may not be able to get rid of my clingy self."

This time when he moved away, it was to take her lips in a soft kiss. He would keep it tender and refuse the passion waiting to unleash itself on her.

"What makes you think I'd want to do that?"

"A big, bad rockstar like you wanting to cuddle with the..."

She stopped speaking, immediately raising his suspicions. What was she hiding from him this time? He pulled away again, far enough so he could see that he was right. She avoided his gaze, her shoulders and spine suddenly tense under his hands.

"One thing we *will* talk about tonight is that we will not keep secrets from each other. Nothing is taboo, no subject is too hard, and anything that's painful, we'll help each other to bear. But I need to know that you'll be as open with me as I will be with you going forward, love." When she looked at him, he continued. "So how about you finish that sentence for me, hmm? It feels like a weighty ending was coming and you cut it off. I want to know why you think 'a big, bad rockstar' like me wouldn't want to cuddle with you."

She shifted her gaze to his chest before she spoke. "You can have any *experienced* woman that you want."

He heard the emphasis, and it took him a second to understand what she was saying. Shock reverberated through him ... she was a virgin? *Fuck me!* How was he supposed to respond to that? It couldn't have been easy for her to admit it in the first place, and to do so to a man who had just told her he was pursuing her must have been just this side of humiliating.

And yet, how much courage had it taken for her to break that wall of silence enough to admit that? In his experience, people beyond a certain age hid their continued virginity fiercely, as if it were a shameful, dirty secret. He never understood that. Every person in the world had a timetable for when things got done and none were alike. It seemed such a waste of emotional energy to fret about what anyone thought about something as personal as when someone lost his or her virginity.

"Chrissy, I'm glad that you felt you could trust me with your secret, but you need to know that it doesn't matter to me. I'm not looking for experience. I'm looking for connection. And we're building that. Please don't spend another minute fretting about your lack of experience. I promise you that if that's what you want, I can help you with that, okay?"

The smile that broke over her face like the sun after a rainstorm warmed him. "Okay."

He pulled her in again, hugging her tightly. Dropping another soft kiss on her head, he moved away and stood up.

"May I have this dance?"

She took the hand he extended to her and moved into his arms as though she belonged there. Oh, for that to be true! He swayed gently with her, letting the music flow over them. She held him tentatively until he wrapped his arms around her and pulled her closer. Then she took the hint and draped her own around his neck, smiling up at him when he said, "That's much better."

He led her in a circle around the coffee table and joined her when she began to hum quietly. She really did have a lovely voice.

"Do you enjoy singing?"

"I do. My aunts sent me for voice lessons for a while, and I loved it. My tutor had concerts, and I sang solos and was a part of his exhibition choir as well."

The pride in her voice made his heart swell. "So you could possibly give me a run for my money then, huh?" he teased.

She snorted. "I very much doubt that. For starters, I'd have to have way more presence than I do, and being on stage terrifies me."

"I thought you said you sang solos?"

"That doesn't mean I wasn't frightened out of my wits. But my aunts also taught me how to show a great poker face. The singing was never the issue. The people staring at me were." She paused and looked up at him again. "How do you manage it? Have you *ever* had stage fright?"

"I've never had stage fright, exactly, but the lead-up to every performance gives me anxiety until I actually start to sing. So, not fright. I can't really see many individuals when I'm on stage, so I suppose that helps. But the first song always lifts me above the anxiety, and after that, it's a breeze."

"Is that why you always sing something energetic to start?"

He grinned. "You're a smart cookie, aren't you? Yes, that's exactly why. It helps to break the tension, so everything is easy after that."

If only the same could be said for what he was trying to build a second time with her. The first time he had crashed and burned. He was determined to find out where he'd lost out, because this time, he intended to win.

CHAPTER 7

"Earth to Chrissy!"

Antonia Larson's—no, Antonia McLaren's—amused voice, accompanied by her snapping fingers, roused Chrissy from her trance. They were at lunch, and Toni had been regaling her with stories from her honeymoon. She had no idea when she had stopped listening and started daydreaming, but there it was.

"Sorry! I'm glad you had a good time."

"Don't think you're going to get away without telling me where you just went in your head, missy! I'm on to you. Something's up. We have fifteen minutes before we need to get back to work. Spill."

Where to begin? So much had happened in the last three weeks since Toni had gotten married and gone on honeymoon with her hunky husband. Her own reconciliation with Rory had begun at the reception, and it had ramped up in the following week. And now, two weeks into his UK mini tour, they were texting daily, and he called her every night right after the show. And then there was the whole "becoming more open" experiment. Maybe she should start there.

But before she could speak, Toni added, "It must be pretty heavy if it's taking you this long to figure out how to tell me."

"It's ... well, it's not heavy exactly. More..." she hunted for the right word. "Momentous, maybe? Life changing?" *Way to sound like a drama llama, Chrissy!* "I've decided that I need to get out more, that it's time to make more friends."

"You mean more than me?" Toni chuckled. "Amen to that! Not that I don't enjoy your friendship, love, but what will you do when I'm not around?"

"What do you mean? Are you going somewhere?" She would not let her anxiety at that prospect leak into her voice. Poker face, remember? Poker voice was also a thing.

"No, I'm just saying. You need more than me. So how are you going to go about getting out there?"

"Well, the other admin assistants go out once a month to a club, and I've decided I'll join them. They invite me every time, but I always find some reason to refuse."

Toni laughed. "I'll bet you shocked the pants off them when you said yes this time."

"I did. Moira kept looking over at me like I had two heads. Jeff outright asked me if I was feeling alright."

Toni's laughter grew. "So when's this happening?"

"Tomorrow night." She was already worrying about what to wear to work, since they'd be going there straight after.

"So what brought this on?"

Trust Toni to get right to the real issue. This was the heart of the matter. Since that night at Rory's place, when she had confessed her lack of experience, Chrissy had made an important decision. She would do everything she could to grow beyond her fears and anxieties, to become the strong, brave woman that Rory thought she was. And it had to begin with her learning to live for more than her job and her cats.

She had moved away from everything that was familiar and safe for a reason, and after almost two years, it was time she lived up to the hype she tried to sell to her aunts every time she went home. She needed to be the smart, worldly, engaging woman she admired in others. And that would only happen if she left her cocoon.

"Rory and I had a date just before he went on tour," she began. "It just became clear to me that I need to be *more* ... you know, to be better."

Toni's face grew serious. "Are you doing this for Rory? Because if you are, that's the wrong reason. You should only be changing for yourself. *You* are the only person who matters. If doing this will make you happy, then go for it. But if you're only doing this to make Rory happy..."

"No, it's not like that at all." How could she explain? "I really want to change because I realize that I can't be all I want to be if I don't move.

Being the kind of person Rory is into will just be a cool bonus."

Toni drained her glass of lemonade and smiled. "Then I wish you a lot of success. Go forth and discover your worldlier inner woman."

Chrissy chuckled as she finished her own drink. It was a relief to speak the words aloud, to have someone she trusted hear her intention. And while she had always known she would do it for herself, it was affirming to have Toni repeat it for her. This wasn't about Rory. This was about her.

Not that that helped her choose what to wear when she got home from work that night. Her usual uniform of straight-legged black slacks and a black blazer over a white silk shell would also likely need to change. She had bought a new suit for work a month ago but hadn't worn it as yet. She'd been waiting for the right time. It seemed like tomorrow would be the right time. She pulled the suit from the wardrobe, still in its plastic wrapping, and held it up to the light.

The skinny trousers had looked good on her when she'd tried them on in the store. Stopping just above the ankles, they drew attention to her toned calves and thighs, and to her wide hips and round bottom. It was not a look she had ever cultivated, but she hadn't been able to resist them in the store. What better way to start on her new persona than to wear something that was at once familiar and completely different? She'd wear the soft pink shell that she had seen it staged with in the store as well. In for a penny, in for a pound, as they say.

Rory called later as she was settling into bed. She loved their nightly conversations, which always happened right after the show, in deference to her earlier rising time each morning. They were innocuous enough, mostly about the concert, which song he'd done first, what the groupies had tried this time, and all the usual post-concert chaos.

"Are you ready for tomorrow?" he asked, after making her laugh along with him at the shenanigans that he and the band had gotten up to in Liverpool earlier that day.

"I've chosen what to wear, if that's what you mean."

"Send me a photo from the club. I want to see you in it."

So far, he had been the one sending her shots of him or the others taken by their photographer or by fans. In one shot, he'd been a sweaty mess after the second encore, and she'd wanted to reach out and wipe his brow. What would it be like to go on tour with him for a few shows and not just a single concert? To be the one who made his recovery smoothie or who was his soft place to land when the night was over? She had a secret wish to witness the whole process, from rehearsals to the after-show madness.

There was a kind of energy that emanated from the group when they performed, as if their fairy godmother had waved a wand over them and blessed them with magic. The one concert she'd been to had been electric, and everything that she had seen had only added to that perception. Power crackled in the air around them as they sang and played, power and a kind of sensuality that made her skin tingle and an answering current of awareness sink in down to her core.

"I'm sure it won't be as exciting as any of the shots you've sent me, but I'll do it if you're sure."

"I'm sure." He stifled a yawn. "Sorry. Today was longer than usual, and tonight's audience demanded three encores. Bossy Liverpudlians!"

He laughed as he said it, and she joined him. "Have you had your smoothie as yet? You told me you have one every night so your body can replenish itself while you sleep."

"I'm having it now, love. Thanks for remembering."

She managed not to tell him that she remembered everything he said to her. The new Chrissy was not going to be a simpering fool.

"Well then, I'd better let you get to bed, hadn't I? If memory serves, you'll be in Manchester next, right?"

"Swotting the itinerary, are you?"

She liked it when he teased her, and she was emboldened to respond in kind. "Only if there's an exam at the end."

"I think you've already passed any test I might want to give you," he answered, his voice suddenly hoarse.

She didn't know how to answer that, so she kept silent, breathing a sigh of relief when he added, "I'll call you tomorrow night, but I expect pictures before then."

"I promise. Goodnight, Rory."

"Good night, little kitten."

Solstice, the club the others took her to, was already filling up when they got there. The flashing lights and loud music would have been more intimidating if they hadn't prepared Chrissy beforehand. She followed them to the second level, which was relatively quiet, though the music from the first floor still echoed around them. Up here, there were still tables available for groups who came together.

"Right, first round's on the newbie," Jeff, the executive assistant to all the members of the senior leadership of Hope House, said. "So don't you all go ordering the most expensive drinks. We want her to come back, right?"

They had already warned her that that was the tradition, so the group cheered, making Chrissy grin. She was enjoying the lighthearted teasing and the corresponding emotions fizzing like shaken soda in a can inside her.

"Thanks, Jeff. I appreciate you." He had to know, being one of the most senior among them, that she wasn't made of money quite yet.

Once they'd all decided what they wanted to drink—she had chosen to try a Paloma—Jeff raised a hand and a server approached almost immediately to take their orders. After he'd left, Sandy, who worked with the social workers, turned to her.

"I'm so glad you came out with us, Chrissy," she said. "I know it's loud, but it's a lot of fun, especially after a drink or two."

"I'm not much of a drinker," Chrissy replied, "but I'm sure I'll have a good time, anyway."

She could do young and vibrant, like her coworkers, even if it meant loosening herself up with a couple of drinks. She didn't plan to get drunk or even tipsy, but since she had no idea of what her alcohol tolerance levels were, it paid to be cautious until she was more comfortable. She had heard enough horror stories about what could happen to folk in nightclubs, and she wasn't about to do anything foolish, even if the people she was with were doing their best to befriend her.

"How did you all find this place?" she asked, looking around her at the space.

It was large, with glittering disco balls suspended on stout metal poles from the high ceiling over the dance floor just below the eye level of the guests on the balcony. Sconces set high into the walls at intervals offered muted lighting on the second floor. The dance floor on the lower level was jammed with a rowdy crowd that seemed to grow larger every time she looked down over the railings onto the scene below.

"Blake has a membership and invited us all to his engagement party, which they held here in the members' section," Andrea, seated in one of the chairs, replied.

Jeff, who was seated on her other side, asked, "How long have you been at Hope House?"

"Eighteen months." Saying it that way made the time seem longer than it was.

"So why have you been keeping to yourself then? Us plebs not good enough for ya?"

Chrissy searched his unsmiling face and almost missed the twinkle in his eye. She chuckled.

"You're a cheeky bugger, aren't you?"

Jeff feigned ignorance. "Whatever do you mean? I'm an angel of God," he deadpanned.

Andrea, on his other side, burst out laughing. She was a Jamaican who had lived in England most of her life. "As my mum would say, 'Mine lightnin'!'" She broke out the heavy accent, making Chrissy marvel. Most days, no one would know that Andrea hadn't been born English.

Jeff broke, cackling like a demented witch. "Your mum scares me. I'd rather she didn't call down God's lightning on me, thank you very much!" He turned to Chrissy and added, "When her mum tells you to watch out for lightning, you've been caught in a fib, and if you don't watch yourself, you'll be in the doghouse."

Andrea laughed. "Jeff thinks my mum works magic."

"Don't sugarcoat it. I'm nae ashamed to say I think her mum's into that voodoo stuff." Chrissy heard the lilt creep into his voice and his expression was earnest and playful at the same time.

"Isn't voodoo Haitian folklore, not Jamaican?" Chrissy asked, turning to Andrea. "Wouldn't your mum have to be an obeah woman?"

Andrea laughed. "Whoa, Jeff! You've been schooled." Her tone was approving.

Jeff wasn't even a bit embarrassed. "What other trivia gems do you have hidden under your hat then, lass? Maybe we should recruit you for our trivia pub quiz nights as well?"

The server arrived with their drinks just then, and once they'd all taken their own, and Chrissy had taken a cautious sip of hers—*Mmm!*

Delicious!—Sandy immediately jumped on Jeff's last comment.

"If we *did* get her to join us for quiz night, she wouldn't be on your team, mate. She'd be with us girls." The s on us sounded like z the way she said it.

"How is that fair?" Jeff protested. "There's only us two blokes." His tone was one of injured outrage. Chrissy had had no idea that he was such a card.

As though he had been conjured, a tall, burly man walked up to their table carrying two glasses and escorting a woman who matched him in height and physical beauty. The man Chrissy knew was Blake, whose boss was the head of security. The beauty must be his wife. *I was right that Mr. United Kingdom would only have a gorgeous wife.* He pulled out the only remaining chair for his wife, then shooed Sandy closer to Chrissy so he could sit at the end of the booth next to her.

"Evening, everyone." He took the woman's hand and introduced her. "This is my wife, Grace. Grace, these are my workmates."

He introduced each of them, and once all greetings were made, he took a long sip of his drink. Then he looked around him before settling his gaze on Chrissy.

"It's good to see you out and about, Christina," he said. "Finally got up the nerve, eh?"

"She was just about to tell us why she never came out with us before, but now you've said that..." Jeff eyed her suspiciously. "Did we scare you? Did *I* scare you? What on earth did I do? And why didn't you say something, lass?"

When he was feeling strong emotion, Jeff's natural Scottish brogue broke free just a little bit, and it always tickled Chrissy, though no one but she knew that. Now she smiled at him, feeling a little mischievous, though she didn't want to cause him too much unnecessary distress.

"I don't know, Jeff. Maybe I didn't say anything because I was a bit intimidated?"

She could couch the truth in a teasing response that they might take seriously or not, but she hoped it would get them off the subject. She was here now, and so far, they'd been having fun, so she could see herself doing it again. Besides, if she planned to hang out with Rory and his band, she'd have to practice her socializing-outside-of-a-nun's-home skills. Might as well do it with this lot whom she already knew.

Clearly her poker face was nowhere near as good as Jeff's because he burst out laughing. "*Now* who's a cheeky bugger, eh, lass?"

"Me? I never!"

She tried to play his innocent act, but broke into more laughter when he winked at her, shaking her head at him. He had been the first to invite her out with the group, and he was the one who most often sought her out just to ask how she was doing and to offer his help if she ever needed it. He was a couple of years younger than she was, and if she didn't know better, she'd think he wanted more from her than friendship.

However, according to the grapevine—which she was privy to even if she never contributed to it—Jeff was nursing a grieving heart. His older lover had died recently, and these monthly get-togethers with his friends probably got him out of the home they had shared more than he might otherwise have done. She was glad that she had helped make him smile by finally being bold and accepting their invitation. He was a kind man, and he deserved to be happy at least some of the time. And if she could help him make it happen, well, that was all to the good.

"Second round, everyone?"

Jeff was apparently the chief of their little band of mates, and since no one seemed to mind him taking charge, Chrissy let him get on with it. She decided she'd try another new drink and perused the online menu before going with the Old Fashioned because there was sugar in it. She didn't know if she'd like the whisky, but she didn't have to finish it if she didn't like it, right? Her cheeks heated when she realized that the server was patiently waiting for her to place her order.

"Sorry. I'll have an Old Fashioned, please."

"I hope you didn't drive here," Blake said when the second round was served.

She cocked a brow at him. "Why?" she asked curiously. Only a couple of them knew that she didn't drive.

"Mixing different kinds of alcohol is a recipe for impairment." He sounded like she imagined a big brother or a dad would sound, stern and worried.

"I took a cab," she told him, needing to relieve his concern. "But don't worry, this will likely be my last experiment for the night. It'll be ginger ale after this until I leave."

"Nothing wrong with being a cream puff, lass," Jeff teased.

"At least they taste good," she retorted without thinking, then felt her cheeks heat as she realized how her response could be interpreted.

She couldn't have Jeff thinking she was flirting with him, but at the same time, she didn't know what to do to fix it. Backpedaling now would make it too obvious where her head had gone, and she didn't need anyone else knowing that she often wondered what it would be like to have a man taste her everywhere. Biting the inside of her cheek—because who thought about things like that in company?—she hurried on.

"I told you I don't know how I react to large amounts of alcohol, and I'm not planning on finding out tonight."

"Smart girl," Andrea chimed in approvingly. "Save *that* for our girls' night out."

What? Was she ready to be with women other than Toni? She knew, from hearing them talk in the break room, that they could be very catty, and she always pitied whoever they happened to be discussing. If they ever talked about her, she was glad she hadn't overheard it, and she wasn't keen to give them any reason to start now by giving them the means to gather the dirt on her that would fuel their gossip.

She slid a non-committal smile on her face and looked over at Grace, who had been studying her closely for a little while. Something about her seemed familiar, but Chrissy couldn't figure out what it was.

"Do you know Sister Mary Clare? From Ely?"

Chrissy almost choked on the sip of drink she had just taken. That was definitely the last question she had expected to be asked in a nightclub in London on a random Friday night after work.

CHAPTER 8

"Interview in an hour, Rory."

Sam Keswick, the band's agent and manager, stopped by where Rory was sitting alone, finishing the chocolate bar he'd opened the previous night and re-reading Chrissy's last text, added after the two photos she'd sent per his request. The girl was a knockout when she smiled, and he'd bet she had no clue. He had crashed for the night after a brief convo where he could swear something was off with her, but he couldn't figure out what it was.

He nodded absently at Sam, too focused on the words to notice the organized chaos unfolding around him in the room.

I didn't remember her at all, she'd written. *What are the chances that I'd meet someone from my past—whom I never really knew—in a club in London the first time I went out to one? And who'd think she'd not only know my aunts but would also remember me?*

Rory had to agree. That was definitely some kind of weird serendipity. He wished he could call her because something told him she was not as calm as she'd wanted him to believe. But there hadn't been time after their brief talk. How would he feel in her situation? Most of the lads from his teen years were merely memories at this point. He'd only kept in touch with a few, two of them being now members of his band.

She hadn't responded to his comment as yet, but he knew she was probably just getting to work, and there would be no time to call her before late afternoon unless the soundcheck was seamless. Since that wasn't a given, he'd have to temper his curiosity—and if he were being honest, his worry—until there was time.

"You're too old to have chocolate for breakfast," Sam added. "We have a long day before sound-check. We can't have you passing out before the show starts again, so please don't add to my stress. Eat something proper, Rory!"

Rory shook his head ruefully. Would he ever live that down? "I was ill, you twat!" His tone held no malice, and Sam laughed.

"That's your excuse, is it?"

"I was!" he protested.

"That's no excuse for letting yourself get dehydrated in the desert!"

Okay, so that *had* been stupid of him. To be sick in all that terrible heat was bad enough, but to not have any food or drink for almost sixteen hours had been disastrous. He was lucky that someone had been there to catch him before he fell and hit his head. Adding concussion to that mix would have been a hot mess.

"I'll eat, Mother. Stop fussing!"

Sam gave him the rude two-fingered salute and he chuckled. He was blessed to work with people who saw the real him and who did their best to treat the man behind the star with affection and care. He pocketed his phone and walked over to where a breakfast buffet had been laid out.

"Proteins, Mr. Fit," Will, his longtime friend, fellow vocalist, and whiz on the lead guitar, whispered in his ear.

"What? Sam doesn't trust me?" Rory turned to eye him. "I do know what a proper breakfast is, you know."

Will chuckled without replying, loading his plate full of eggs, bacon, sausage, and a minuscule helping of beans.

"What, no toast?" Rory teased, knowing full well how Will hated "burnt bread," as he called it.

"Sod off, wanker!"

Both men laughed at the good-natured insult and went over to one of the two tables set aside for the purpose. The food was good, and Rory was ravenous, so he ate everything he'd put on his plate, which hadn't been much, and he sat contemplating whether or not to go back for seconds.

"You know, I've never understood why you eat like a bird, Ro." Will's comment broke into his vacillating. "I mean, there isn't even an ounce of spare flesh on you, man."

"Stalker!"

Rory would rather not have his best friend taking too much stock of his appearance because if he brought it up even casually, Sam was sure to jump all over it, and the next thing he knew, he'd be on a special diet to beef him up. He didn't need beefing up, as they'd all know if they came to his workouts with him. He already had his hands full with Sam mother-henning him after that whole fainting thing. He didn't need him monitoring what he actually ate when he did eat.

"Friends never let friends starve themselves. Here, give me that."

Before Rory could protest, Will had picked up his plate and was heading back towards the food-laden tables.

"Hey! Stop right there! I can get what I want."

Rory grabbed at his arm as he walked by, but Will ignored him. He made a rude noise with his lips instead.

"I could see you talking yourself out of going for seconds," he said. "I'm just winning the argument for your good angel."

Rory shook his head, chuckling at his friend's madness. John joined him at the table, his own plate full.

"Done already?" he asked, shoveling a forkful of food into his mouth.

"Mother dearest has gone to get me seconds." He gestured toward Will, who had reached the table and was choosing food for him. "Apparently, I eat like a bird." He rolled his eyes for good measure.

"Well, you are a picky eater, aren't you?"

"Not you, too, Beats. I am *not*..."

"The rocker doth protest too much, methinks." John swallowed some of his tea and took another huge bite of food, his eyes twinkling with mirth.

"Instead of waxing Shakespearean on me, why don't we talk about today's schedule, huh? That's a far more practical use of our time."

Will returned just then, and Rory eyed the toast and jam and the extra slices of bacon on the plate with a grin. Trust Will to know exactly what would hit the spot for him the second time around. They'd been friends so long that most people thought, at one time or another, that they were together.

"Brilliant, mate! Thanks."

"So how's your girl?"

Rory couldn't stop the way the corners of his mouth lifted. Just the mention of Chrissy, even if not by name, brought a smile to his cheeks.

"She's fine. She went out to a club with her workmates last night."

Will raised a surprised brow. "I thought you said she was a homebody."

"I said she grew up sheltered and wasn't much for partying." Rory felt forced to correct his friend.

"Six o' one, half a dozen o' the other." Will shrugged. "Did she have a good time?"

"She did."

He wasn't about to speculate on his suspicions regarding the blast from her past with people who didn't really know her, even though they were his friends.

"Let's go, boys. The limo's here."

Sam's strident call cut the conversation short. They drained their teacups, and Rory stuffed the last bit of bacon and jammed toast into his mouth, grabbing a napkin to wipe his lips when he was done. Hopefully, there'd be bottled water in the car. A last swish before he faced the people in the radio station was necessary. By the time they were all shown into the studio where their host was waiting, he had buried all thoughts of Chrissy so he could focus on the work.

"Gentlemen, good morning. I'm Grant Webster. Welcome to "Manchester in the Morning." Our fans have been anxiously awaiting your arrival, as have I, to be honest."

"Thanks for inviting us."

Rory was usually the one to answer general comments for the band. They had a routine down for how to field questions,

"So how has the mini tour been so far? According to your itinerary, you've already hit five cities across the northern UK."

"Indeed, we have." Henry, their rhythm guitarist and one of the backup vocalists, answered next. "And we've had a grand time in each of them. The fans were so welcoming, and the energy was exceptional. The Liverpudlians were even bossy enough to demand three encores!"

They all laughed at that, and Rory noticed how genuine amusement softened the hard lines on Grant's face.

"Your band has a signature sound that makes old and young alike swoon. Between the brilliant lyrics and the stellar performances, you've stolen the hearts of countless numbers of fans across the world. How do you account for your continuing success?"

Rory always loved questions about the music. "It's really important to us to work with authentic emotion, you know? Love, anger, rage, fear ... they're all the stuff that makes our music resonate with folks."

"Too true, Riordan. And some of your love songs have become almost cult classics. Songs like 'Not Just Today' and 'Let Me Love You' have remained in the top twenty for months at a time. What are your personal favorites?"

Each of them named a couple of tunes, some of them overlapping. The interview continued, running through the usual questions about their upcoming US tour, including asking which city across the pond they were most excited to be performing in and which one they'd never been to before.

All easy questions, really, until Grant said, "So Riordan, as you know, your fans are always on the lookout for gossip about your love life."

Rory tensed. He had never been a fan of personal questions, though he'd always done his best to be as open as he could be without giving away anything important. Where the hell was this heading?

"Rumor has it that you've reconnected with someone special whom we haven't seen around for a few months." Grant held his gaze unblinkingly for a long moment before adding, "What can you tell us about that? Is there someone special, and if so, who is she? No one seems to know anything about her, not even her name, and your bandmates all clam up every time anyone asks them."

Rory looked around at his mates with a smile of thanks. They knew enough to know he wouldn't have appreciated a leak of any kind from them, and they also knew how leery Chrissy was of the limelight.

"It must be clear to you, Grant, that we have each other's backs." He looked at his mates again. "Thanks, guys." Then he looked back at Grant. "As to the rumor, I can neither confirm nor deny it, especially since I don't know where it's coming from. There are a few people with whom I've reconnected in the past twelve months, none of whom would appreciate me making a spectacle of them in the press."

"Of course, I understand your reluctance to expose people's private lives to press scrutiny, Riordan, but surely you understand the way it works for public figures such as yourself? Fans have an unquenchable need to know everything about you ... about all of you, in fact." He pinned each of them in turn with his gaze.

"That's as may be," Will answered for them, "but as I'm sure you know from personal experience, we don't always get everything we want, do we? I mean, I want an audience with the King, but that's not very likely, is it?"

A burst of laughter from the group eased the tension in Rory's shoulders. However, he'd been put on notice now, and from here on, he'd be more cautious.

Grant chuckled wryly at the pointed rejection of his and their fans' curiosity about Rory's life. He was a journalist; he knew the score. He turned his attention to John, who didn't care *who* knew about his romantic life.

"How's engagement been treating you, John? We were all chuffed to hear the good news, even though some of your fans are weeping in their cups for their lost opportunity."

John laughed. "My lady and I are beyond happy, thank you very much. Best of luck to everyone looking for their person, though. I really believe there's someone out there for everyone."

"From your mouth to God's ears, John," Grant said with a chuckle, though it seemed to Rory that there was a wistful look in his eyes as he continued. "Set a date for the big day as yet?"

John raised his hands in a gesture of surrender. "I'm leaving all that up to her. I'll do my part to make sure I get to keep her forever, but she gets the tough stuff. I admit it … I'm lazy and scared of wedding planners."

Even the crew working the show laughed uproariously at that. Rory loved that John was so open, so free, so unaffected. That was his way of ensuring that no drama was attached to his name. If you thought you knew everything, what was there to make a scandal about when everything was on the up and up? Only the band members and his family knew the few things that he trusted them to keep out of the public eye.

Grant looked down at his tablet, then looked up again.

"As all your fans know, your band is called Third Generation because each of you is a third, yes?"

Nods all around. No need for anyone to speak. Any online search would answer that question.

"The assumption has always been that if one is a third, then he comes from a family of means. What is it like to be the heir apparent, as it were, to wealthy fathers? We've had a number of fans ask about your relationships with your families, particularly with your dads. Any comment on that?"

Henry took that one. He knew that neither Rory nor Tristan, their bassist, talked about their fathers since—among other things—both had difficult relationships with them. They all also knew where the question was coming from. There had been a proper row between Tristan and his dad that had made the papers where his family lived in Sussex. It had only been a matter of time before it hit social media, and then there was no stopping it.

"Not that there's anything for most of us to inherit, so that pressure is off of us, but there's really nothing to tell there. We're just a bunch of boring almost-forty-year-old guys who enjoy the work we do and who have the love and support of the people in our lives. And if you're referring to the stories on social media about what happened between our bassist and his dad, I *would* defer to him on that, except I know he will say, and I quote, 'No comment.'" He turned to look at Tristan. "Am I right, mate?"

Tristan nodded, his expression one of studied neutrality. Henry continued. "So there's no more drama, except when our mums complain that we don't visit often enough and threaten dire punishments that scare none of us. But that's something all mums of grown men do, isn't it?

More laughter greeted that last comment. That's why they loved Henry. He knew exactly how to say nothing in such a way as to make it appear to be something. And even though it was an evasion, his answer was so skillfully worded that unless Grant asked each of them a specific question, there was nowhere else to go with it.

Apparently, Grant agreed with Rory's silent assessment, because he moved on.

"You've all been together for almost fifteen years now, and your reputation has grown exponentially. It's no secret that at least on this side of the pond, and in Europe as a whole, you've all done extremely well for yourselves. The accolades and awards you've earned speak for themselves ... two ARIA awards for Best International Artist, three Grammy nominations, one for Best Album and two for Best Rock Song, and three BRIT Awards for Song of the Year and for Songwriter of the Year. Where do you see Third Generation headed after your American tour next year? Rumors have been flying on social media about the future of the band."

This was a trick question and Rory knew it. Henry, who was the one to pay attention to the band's social media page for the rest of them, kept them in the loop about any and all rumors that showed up on all the online platforms where they had a presence and a fan base. A few had been flying around lately about the band breaking up.

None of them knew when, how, or why that had become a thing, and they had had many conversations about how to address it, particularly since it was skirting a significant truth that they were keeping hidden for the moment. They weren't breaking up, just considering what it would be like if they cut back on touring and did more studio work going forward. No decision had been made, and they didn't plan to say anything until their decision was firm.

"Well, obviously, we'd love to actually *win* a Grammy next time, Grant." Nods and grins from his bandmates accompanied Rory's response. "But we're taking it year by year," he added. "We've got long-term tours planned for the next couple of years, and we're already in negotiations for events in the two after that. So the short answer is that we see ourselves being extremely busy going forward."

"So just to be clear, the band is *not* breaking up?"

"That is correct." Rory rolled his inner eye at the man. "Was that the rumor you were referring to?"

As if he didn't already know the answer. He just had to make it clear that two could play the game the host was playing.

"It was indeed." Grant slanted a knowing smile at Rory, as if to acknowledge that he knew what he'd just done. "So according to your posted itinerary, you're in five more cities over the next two weeks, ending back in London. Any rest for the weary after this whirlwind tour?"

"We have a few other gigs coming up." Tristan finally spoke. "But for the most part, we'll be resting and working on our next studio album. If you're in London in a fortnight, you should definitely come and see us. We'll be debuting a couple of new singles then."

He was the most reserved of the band members, and he seemed happiest when he could give the end of the interview spiel. It meant he had contributed, which was something they had all agreed that everyone needed to do. They were a team, and they wanted to present a united front at all times.

The interview wrapped up after that, and after thanks and goodbye handshakes, they were off to one of the local television stations for another shorter interview and performance of a new song from their next album. They had an hour to get there, retouch makeup, and warm up their voices before the show, which was a Graham Norton-style show, just at mid-morning. Instead of adult beverages, they'd be offered coffee, tea, crumpets, scones, and butter or jam once their section ended.

On the way, Rory made a quick call to Chrissy, not expecting her to answer since it was almost ten in the morning. He was preparing to leave her a flirty message when she picked up.

"Rory? Are you alright?"

The worry in her voice knocked him for six. Only his mother ever assumed that something was wrong if he called her at an unexpected time, and he knew it came from a place of love.

"I'm fine, love. I just wanted to say hello."

"Thank you."

He could hear the smile in her voice. *This ... this is what I want, for her to be happy because I made her smile.*

"I wanted to ask you about last night. Did something happen with Grace?" He waited patiently for her answer.

"Not really," she said eventually. "I was just taken aback, that's all. She's a little older than I am and apparently, she used to visit us sometimes with her mum, who's my Aunt Clare's friend. She remembered me almost immediately, but it took me a minute to place her."

"That doesn't explain why you seemed so bothered by it, love," he prodded gently.

He wanted to know the whole story, but they were pulling into the parking lot of the television station. "I have to go now, but when I call you later, we'll finish this conversation. Just promise me that you're okay now."

She chuckled. "I promise, Rory. I'm fine."

Inside, they were immediately led into the studio, set up for their on-air interview, where they awaited their host, Benedict Mason. The man who walked in after ten minutes could have been mistaken for a GQ model, what with his height and build and tanned good looks. His suit was clearly bespoke, and the watch adorning his manly wrist was a bulky, showy thing that added to the whole impact of his presence. Even his cologne, though understated, was award-winning. Rory thanked heaven for being given a consummate professional, even if the man's entire aspect was somewhat intimidatingly perfect.

"Ladies and gentlemen, let's give a warm Daytime with Benedict welcome to our special guests Third Generation!"

An enthusiastic round of applause went on for a minute while they waved and smiled. Pleasantries, including highlights from their first five concerts on the tour, were followed by another round of the same old questions, this time with a viewing audience. Thankfully, they didn't have to field any personal questions ... maybe this guy had listened in to the radio show and chosen to avoid being politely shut down.

Their PR person had provided two special gifts from the band, apart from the t-shirts for everyone, for audience members. Once those were handed off—one by Rory to a woman so overcome with emotion that she bawled when he hugged her, and the other by Tristan to a cute teenager who was clearly as shy as Tris, which made their selfie even sweeter—they sang their latest single, "Hunger," to end the interview. It was passionate and sensual and filled with emotions they had all experienced.

As Rory sang, his thoughts went to Chrissy, to the way he craved her, and if his tone was extra deep the further into the song he went, well, that was only to be expected.

> "I hunger for the taste of you.
> Deep down,
> where longing waits untapped,
> I crave the flavor of you."

He wished she could see him now.

CHAPTER 9

"It was definitely a surprise, Aunt Clare."

Chrissy dried the last of the few dishes she had used for dinner, and once she'd put them away, she picked up the cell phone that she had propped against the toaster and walked into the lounge. The cats had taken over the couch, so she sat on the loveseat and curled her legs up under her while her aunt continued to muse aloud.

"I had no idea that Grace had been married. The last I heard she was engaged. How long has she been married, then?"

"I don't know for sure, Aunt Clare, but I think it's been at least a year."

"Well, if that girl could find a man to marry, your aunty and I have nothing to worry about you. She was the quietest little thing."

Chrissy chose to ignore the comment about her getting married. That was not likely to happen with the way she was currently without a man in her life. She refused to count Rory, because there was nothing between them except a regrowing friendship. What was she, stupid? She knew better than to count her chickens before they hatched.

"I don't really remember much about her, Auntie."

"I'm not surprised. Neither of you was very good at making friends, were you? She'd come and spend the whole time glued to her mother's elbow, while we had a hard time getting you to stay in the room for more than five minutes. One time Zelda had to physically bring you back into the lounge from the kitchen where you'd scuttled off to like some frightened rabbit."

Her aunt's amused chuckle was rare enough that it made Chrissy smile to hear it. She had always been the more austere of the two nuns, and Chrissy supposed part of it had to do with the fact that all she had ever known from the time she was eighteen were the strictures of living with a bunch of other women whose entire existence was devoted to the service of God and others, and who only understood a life of monastic isolation and self-denial.

"She's not shy anymore, Auntie."

Grace had been more than a stylish attachment to her husband's arm. She'd been charming, personable, witty, and friendly. That was actually what had left Chrissy feeling less sure of herself than before in a place she'd never been to with people she barely knew. What did she have in common with any of *them*, when she didn't even have anything in common with the graceful, elegant, self-possessed woman from her past?

"Well, there's hope for you yet."

Chrissy sighed. Her aunt was not known for her tact, especially with family, so she knew better than to take offense at her words, but they still stung. Was she really such a hopeless case? Had she made her aunts worry about her because of how she was? And more to the point, what could she do about it going forward? She knew she needed to change, but it wouldn't be because she was ashamed to be the dull girl her aunts thought she was. It would be because change was important for growth, and that was her goal for the year ... to grow into the kind of woman whom she admired. Confident, radiant, and able to hold her own in a crowd.

"So have you decided when you're coming for another visit? Your Aunt Zelda and I are better now."

"I should be able to come up next weekend, Aunt Clare. I'll let you know which day for sure by the end of the day on Monday."

"Good. It's been too long since we shared tea and crumpets, and Zelda wants to show off her vegetable garden."

Chrissy laughed. "I can't wait, Auntie."

After she hung up, Chrissy switched on the television, searching for something to take her mind off the vaguely troubling conversation with her aunt. She was not *un*happy, exactly, but her cup of contentment was ... empty? Wow! She'd never had *that* thought before. And it didn't make sense to be lacking in contentment and yet be happy ... did it? She was doing what she had dreamed of doing since she was old enough to understand that living with two nuns would not get her to where she thought she might want to be one day, especially because, by temperament, she was already too much like them.

So the time had come for a proper assessment of her emotional status. If she was to become her best self, she had to understand where she was in the moment. Based on the way her aunt's words had disturbed her, she was not happy being single. Nor was she best pleased with being single and unable to change that status because she was disengaged from the world. Clearly, having a good job and living independently were not enough of an enticement for any man to want to be with her.

Rory wants to be with you, her little voice of reason reminded her hopefully. But she didn't trust that. Not yet. They had barely lasted six months before she'd been off and running like a prize stallion at the derby. Rory's interest was not guaranteed to continue if she couldn't manage to get herself together. It was a depressing thought, sending her to the freezer for the remaining few spoonsful of the ice cream she'd been indulging in for the last two nights.

When Rory's call came, she'd just scraped the last bit of chocolate goodness from the container and was contemplating whether or not to use her fingers to get every last spot of the treat from the box before she threw it out. Hastily licking her lips, she answered, glad he couldn't see her.

"Hello?" Why did she sound like she didn't know who was calling? Stupid!

"Chrissy, how are you love?" he asked, as though he knew something was off about her.

"I'm okay." Because she was, honestly. At her age and in her situation, a little emotional insecurity after a talk like the one she'd just had with the woman who had raised her was to be expected, after all.

"Are you sure?" He sounded skeptical. "You sound like you need a hug."

She chuckled ... she couldn't help it. He was either the world's biggest opportunist or he was too intuitive by half.

"Are you sure it's not *you* that needs a hug?" she countered, going with the former explanation for his words.

"I'll never deny wanting your hugs, love," he replied at once. "But that doesn't stop me from recognizing something amiss in your voice."

He paused a moment, then sent the invitation for her to switch to video. She hesitated before switching, schooling her features so nothing showed ... she hoped.

"Hi." She smiled weakly at him, hoping to put him off the scent of her discomfort.

"Hi yourself. Now, are you going to tell me why you're upset, or am I going to have to drop in for a heart-to-heart?"

She looked him full in the eye then. "You can't just drop in and you know it. You're in Sheffield now, aren't you?"

"Yes, the show's tomorrow, then we're on to Birmingham after a rest day. So technically, I *could* drive down to see you and drive back up after."

She wasn't going to let that happen. "I may not be a rockstar, Rory, but I know how taxing being on tour is, especially living out of a bus. So no, you will absolutely *not* drive down to see me and drive back up just because you think something is wrong. I'm fine."

His eyes widened. "Wow! You got quite bossy there, didn't you, love? I think I like it." His words were a low, sensuous purr of sound, and his smile said he wasn't kidding about liking it.

"You're kinky as well as cheeky, aren't you?"

She wasn't sure where this bravado was coming from, but she'd run with it until it fizzled on its own. It was good for her, made her more interesting to the man looking at her with a smirk on his face.

"I can be whatever you need me to be, little kitten."

The weight of a promise lay in his words, despite the grin on his face. He had always been this way ... intensely personal and totally focused on her. Was she ready now to move beyond her fear of his laser-like attention to her? Could she handle the intrusive fans and the glaring lime-light in which he lived any better now than she did before? She had only had a little taste of what being with a rockstar meant for people in his orbit and she hadn't been comfortable with it at all. If she was going to engage with him again, she'd need to answer these questions sooner rather than later.

"So, ready to tell me what happened at the club with your old acquaintance?"

"Nothing happened, honestly, Rory. It's just that meeting Grace again after all these years was eye-opening for me."

He quirked a brow. "How so?"

Chrissy sighed. "According to my Aunt Clare, we were both a bit anti-social as girls, too shy to even make friends with each other. However, the woman I met on Friday night was self-possessed, confident, vivacious, and oozing charm. She's married to a man who is as handsome as she is beautiful, and they're so clearly in love, it was a bit painful to be with them."

He pounced on her sudden silence. "And?"

"Well, I was left feeling like a useless pillock, to be honest. She's only a year older than me, but she's really got her life together. She got over the inhibitions of childhood and snagged herself a hunk of a man who will clearly do anything she asks him to do, and she managed to win over my workmates in one evening. It took me almost a year and a half to spend any time with them outside of work, so I don't know them well at all."

"Neither does she really," he reminded her gently. "She's just had more practice than you, that's all. If you were both shy girls, it was just a matter of opportunity, I'm sure. Maybe she was always that person you met on Friday and only needed life experience to bring it out of her, while you are now who you have always been. Do you think it's fair to compare yourself with her? Isn't that rather like trying to compare apples and oranges?"

His words made sense, and Chrissy wanted to believe them, to trust that he was right and that she wasn't somehow lacking. It was going to be a hard sell, though. She knew who she was. She knew her shortcomings. She knew what was expected and accepted as normal for a woman of her age, and she knew she didn't meet all the prerequisite criteria.

"It doesn't matter anyway. We're not likely to meet again, unless I go out with them again, and I think that that experiment in socializing was a failure."

"I don't understand why you think that, but for the record, some of the sweetest successes are born in failure."

She didn't want him to think that she was a whining drama queen. It wasn't an earth-shattering issue, was it? It was just one awkward woman discovering that she wasn't the social butterfly that she assumed he'd need her to be if they were to be together. She had lowered her eyes from his, and he was having none of it.

"Look at me, Chrissy," he demanded, and waited until she was once again giving him her whole attention. "Anything you choose to do to make you feel more positive about yourself will be great, but please promise me you won't try to be someone you're not. I like you just the way you are, I promise you."

She wasn't sure she liked how that made it sound like she was trying to change for him. She wasn't, and he needed to know that.

"That's as may be, Rory, but I'm not changing for *you*."

Her tone was sharper than she'd meant it to be, but it was too late now to change it. She meant what she'd said, even if the little voice in her head said she wasn't being completely honest. After all, if she wanted to be different so Rory would find her more interesting, wasn't she doing it for him as well? Not the most comfortable question.

"Noted," he answered, his expression unreadable.

Had she offended him? She wished she could ask without making things more awkward than they already were. Time to change the subject.

"What are your plans for your day off then?"

He didn't answer at once, but when he did, his smirk said she hadn't fooled him. "We just need some downtime, so we're taking the morning to go for a spa treatment, then we're out to lunch with the other band who will be our opening act. They're just starting out, but they're very good. It's going to be a great evening. After that, it's the usual."

Chrissy knew that meant one more run-through, soundchecks, setting up the stage, and all the stuff that went into making a concert go without a hitch.

"Well, you know what they say: Break a leg!"

"Thank you." This time his smile was genuinely amused. "I'll do my best not to."

She laughed. His humor eased the tension and relief flooded her body. She hated confrontation, and she hated it even more when it was with Rory. He was her peace. That realization hit her square in the chest, and something must have shown on her face because he frowned at her, his expression now laced with worry.

"Are you alright, love? You look like you had a sudden turn there."

"I'm fine." she hastened to reassure him. "Just gas."

"Have you eaten?"

She grinned. "Yes, Daddy, I have."

His eyes gleamed. "Daddy, huh? Is that something you're interested in pursuing, little kitten?"

She shuddered in disgust. "No, thank you!"

She'd read a few stories in which women in the BDSM community had lovers they called Daddies. She had never had a male parental figure in her life and didn't have any interest in the kind of dynamic that these stories suggested women with Daddies wanted. She wanted an experienced lover, of course, but she wasn't interested in submitting to anyone in the ways it seemed were expected in those types of relationships. She may be inexperienced, but she wasn't a pushover.

Rory laughed at her reaction. "Good to know, little kitten. I'll be sure not to try any of that with you. May I call you in the morning before you go to work?"

Her pulse quickened. "That depends. I wake up at five thirty every morning. I'm guessing you'll still be dead asleep at that hour."

"I can be awake then if that's what you need."

His voice had gone low and rusty, heat and desire leaking through his words like water through a sieve.

"I guess I'll hear from you again in the morning then." She did her best to keep her own voice steady and without inflection, even though the thought of waking up to the sound of his voice made her insides flutter wildly.

"Sleep sweet, love. Tomorrow."

He blew her a kiss and she smiled. "Back at you, Rory."

She wasn't surprised when her cell phone rang at the same moment that the alarm went off the next morning. She'd been awake a few minutes already and had just come back from relieving herself.

"Good morning, Rory," she said, not needing to look to see who was calling.

"Good morning, Chrissy. Did you sleep well?"

"I did, thank you. You?"

"Very well, yes. My dreams were very sweet, which helped." There was a definite laugh in his voice.

"Good for you." She was not touching the dream comment at all.

"What about you? Did *you* have sweet dreams too?"

She could almost see the mischievous waggle of his brows as he spoke. She chuckled. "No. Mine was dreamless again. I guess my life just isn't interesting enough for dreams."

"We'll have to see what we can do about that, won't we?"

"We don't have to do anything about that. Anyway, I need to start getting ready."

"Trying to get rid of me already? We've only just said hello. Don't you want to know what I dreamed about?"

Trouble with a capital T ... that's what this man was. "You'll have to tell me while I make myself some breakfast," she said, heading out to her little kitchen.

"What's for breakfast?"

Was he really that easily distracted, or was he just humoring her? "Two hardboiled eggs, toast, and tea."

She put the phone on speaker, propping it against the bowl of fruit on the kitchen table. Then she set two slices of bread in the toaster but didn't start it and had just pulled the eggs from the refrigerator when he said, "That sounds like a condemned man's breakfast. Or a nun's," he teased.

"It may be." She ignored his ribbing. "But it's easy and filling. Why mess with a good thing?"

"No reason at all, love. But I hope that doesn't mean you never have anything else for breakfast, because I do love a full English breakfast myself."

"Is that what you'll be having later?" She set the eggs on the stove and set the water to boil for her tea.

"I don't know. Depends on how soon I wake up again before the spa appointment."

"Well, you should probably get back to bed then. The more sleep, the better, I always say."

Maybe she could get him off the phone before he recounted his dream because something told her it hadn't been an innocent one. She rinsed out the teapot with hot tap water to warm it up, then added the tea leaves and waited for the water to boil.

"Not before I tell you my dream, little kitten. I dreamed about you. I was singing to you, a new song. That's what woke me up. I had some of the lyrics still in my head when I woke, and I had to write them down before I forgot them."

"That's … very romantic," she said, wondering what he'd been singing to her in his dream, and pleased that apparently, Dream Chrissy inspired songs in a rockstar.

"It was very hot, love. Very. Hot." The last two words, repeated for emphasis, had an overlay of lust that even she could not miss. "I very much wanted to do what I'd been dreaming about, and I wasn't happy when I woke that it was just a dream."

"Aww! I'm sorry, but at least you got a song out of it."

The kettle whistled, and she went to pour the water over the waiting leaves, covering the teapot as she did, and setting the timer for five minutes. When he answered her, it was to ask to see her again. Chrissy looked down at herself. She was wearing a very sensible pair of short pajama bottoms and a slip-on racer-back top with the words "Good at Naps" written over her left breast. She'd not put on her robe because she hadn't thought he'd want to see her so early.

"Just a sec…" she began, but he interrupted her with a request to switch to video.

"No, little kitten, let me see you now. You don't need to do anything. You'll see me, too, just as I am now."

This was such a small thing, and at the end of the day, what would it hurt if he saw her sleep bonnet and the top of her naked shoulders? She could hold the phone where he wouldn't see anything below that. She took a deep breath and switched to video, then gasped softly when she saw Rory, half naked except for a pair of sleep pants with the waistband of his underwear showing—were those boxers or briefs?—his blond hair tousled, a soft smile on his face.

She'd never seen a naked man in the flesh—well, virtually—before. All her exposure to male nudity had been in magazines and on television, and the odd times at the beach, though she hadn't really looked then either. But this was Rory, and the thin layer of hair spread across his defined pecs and sliding down his six-pack into the waistband of his underwear—a darker blond than the color on his head—forming a loose capital T was so inviting she had to restrain herself from her automatic reaction to reach out for a touch. It was a good thing he wasn't actually in the room with her, or she was sure she would have lost the battle.

"You look so sexy, love, all naked shoulders and ... what is that on your head?"

"A sleep bonnet. It's silk and keeps my hair from drying out on the pillowcases, which are cotton, and protects my hair from tangling."

"Red suits you, even if it's on your head," he murmured. "Now, can I see a little bit more of you than the tops of your smooth shoulders? Please?"

"Rory, I don't think..."

"I agree. Don't think. Just show me. I want to see what you're hiding, Chrissy."

Why was it so hard to let him see her pajama top? Aside from the whole seeing my nipples standing at attention because he looks like sex on a stick and his voice is making me wish he was here with me.

"Come on, love, just a quick peek."

Some new demon of daring impulsiveness pricked her hard and she slowly moved the phone down so he could see more of her top, enough so he could see the beginning of the swell of her breast below the teal-colored shirt.

"Mmm. Maybe we can nap together some-time, little kitten. I'm pretty good at naps as well, you know."

His smile was suggestive and mischief-laden, and somehow it helped her relax. She wasn't naked, after all, or flashing him her breasts, and they weren't doing anything too heavily flirtatious. This was more teasing the senses, sharing another personal moment that could lead to deeper ones, if she would allow it. If they'd gone swimming, he would have seen her breasts and legs anyway, even less obscured by cloth than they were at the moment. He'd get an eyeful and then some. Thinking that made her feel even better about allowing the intimacy.

"I'll let you go then. Your tea's getting cold. Enjoy your breakfast, love, and have a good day at work. I'll talk to you later." He blew her a kiss and then added with a wink, "And thank you."

She knew what he meant. "You're welcome."

Because he was. He was welcome to look at her with that same fire of desire in his eyes any time he felt like it.

CHAPTER 10

"You're too quiet, Ro. What's up?"

Rory glanced up, his cup of tea in his hand. He was having a hard time concentrating on anything other than the image of Chrissy, sleep-rumpled and delicious in the tank-top-looking shirt with the cute words above what looked like the swell of breasts. He was going to have to find a way to help her relax around him completely *all* the time.

"Nothing's up. Just tired." He hoped his friend would accept his answer and let it go.

Will studied him critically, cradling the huge mug of coffee in both hands. "You know I don't believe you, right, Ro?" When Rory looked up at him, he smirked. "It's me you're lying to, mate. But I'll leave you alone for now. Seems like this will be a longer conversation than I have time for right now. I scheduled a yoga session before the spa. I'll see you there in an hour."

Rory nodded. "Go be a pretzel then," he said, chuckling. "I'll just go for a run."

Maybe that would clear his head. He needed to move forward with Chrissy, and he and the band needed to decide where they were headed professionally. They'd been doing this since they were in their early twenties, and now, at almost forty, they all felt the need to make some course adjustments. Touring was hard on the mind and body, and with most of them either already being in long-term relationships or contemplating it, they had to figure out how they would fit a healthy family life into their schedules.

He knew once he and the boys made a decision about the band, he'd need to have a proper conversation with his father. It was long overdue, and frankly, he was tired of the standoff. He knew his dad loved him and that his refusal to accept the life Rory had chosen came from a place of concern, not prejudice, but he needed the old man to understand his point of view as well. There had to be a way for him to avoid the cold reception or heated words every time he went home for a visit, or his visits would remain few and far between.

His own relationship status was still in flux, even though he'd told Chrissy what he wanted with her. He would need to keep breaking down her walls, finding ways to romance her that would also build her confidence in herself as a desirable woman. And they'd have to come to some kind of understanding about his life on tour. How did he assure her of his fidelity while on tour when all those stories of his man-whore ways permeated social media, fueled by suggestive but usually photoshopped images of him with women of every tribe and nation?

He understood her reluctance to be with him, he really did, but he would prove to her that he wasn't the person the media made him out to be. Where there was smoke, there was usually a smoke machine operated by paparazzi and journalists out for drama and theatrics. It didn't help that she had firsthand experience of the way women threw themselves at him.

The jogging path he chose wound its way through a small park. It was a short circuit around beautiful flowering beds, an imposing fountain with fish in the moat around it, and cute little park benches set back from the path. He knew he'd need to run quite a few laps before his mind would be quieted. By the time he slowed to a walk to cool down, he'd done twenty laps, which his smartwatch told him had only been three miles. He felt less agitated, though he wasn't as tired as he thought he'd be. Still, he would be late for the sauna if he didn't hurry.

The others were already in the limo waiting when he got back.

"Sorry, lads."

"Did you chase away your demons, mate, or did they chase you?" Henry teased.

"A little bit of both," he said, chuckling. "You know how it is."

"I've arranged for us to use the private entrance because, apparently, our downtime location was leaked to the press, and I know you lads want some freedom this morning."

"How much d'you think it would cost to outfit an American RV as a sauna and massage parlor?"

Was Tris being serious? Rory had no doubt that it could be done, but at what cost? First, they'd have to get the beast to England, and then they'd have to make it meet their needs. That wasn't an expenditure he could see his fellow band members going for. They already had a bus for themselves, one for the crew, and trucks for the instruments and all the other paraphernalia that went into going on tour in the UK. And when they were abroad, they rented those vehicles and stayed in hotels when they could.

"Forget it. We'll just have to keep dealing with loose-lipped individuals as they come and make the best of things."

"What d'you think would be a suitable punishment for the arsehole who gave them the tip off?" Will asked.

"No tips?"

Again, Rory wasn't sure that Tris was being serious, but he looked up with a vehement shake of his head. "No! We don't know if it was any of them who did it, and it wouldn't be fair to the ones who're innocent if we took that away from them to punish someone we can't identify."

"Let it go, boys. Just focus on enjoying the morning. We've got to get our heads back in the game for tonight's show."

Sam firmly shut down the discussion and Rory gladly followed his lead, pulling out his phone and going back to the solitaire game he'd been playing the last time they were traveling. There were still five cities to go, and new songs to debut before they could call this a wrap. And once the tour was over, there would be the big debriefing, because they'd need to know what to do better for the next time.

A couple of the roadies, who were also brothers, had to leave for an emergency back home, and Rory didn't have time to talk to Chrissy for the next few days as he and the other band members spent time making sure the stand-ins got their jobs right. The Brighton and London shows in particular had extra staging required, as well as additional lighting needs, and they wanted everything to go off smoothly, which meant paying extra careful attention to two people who had never worked with them before.

After the Brighton show, which went off without a hitch, they were winding down following their debrief, when John's phone rang. The smile on his face when he checked the caller ID told the rest of the band who was calling, and no one was surprised when he lifted a finger to excuse himself.

"I'll see you all in the morning," he managed to say before he disappeared.

"I think that's our cue to take ourselves off to bed," Will said. "I'm off as well, lads."

Rory settled himself on his bunk and checked the time. It was almost midnight. Had Chrissy gone to bed already? Should he try to call her? He hit speed dial without thinking about it more, and her phone rang once before she picked up.

"Hi, Rory." She sounded adorably sleepy.

"Hi yourself. Did I wake you?" He couldn't be sorry if he had, but he could at least ask.

"Not really. I was just dozing. What's happening? How was the show?"

"It was fantastic! Brighton is always a fabulous place to play. The audience is always a little wild and highly entertaining all by themselves."

"Are you excited to be coming back home?"

There was no inflection in her voice, but Rory couldn't help wondering if she was asking if he was excited to be going home to her. Of course, the answer to that question was a resounding yes. He couldn't wait to see her again. It had been a whole bloody month without her. The phone calls and video chats didn't count because he still hadn't touched her once or felt her breath on him.

"More than you know, love. It's been a long month, even though this was a short tour."

"It'll be nice to see you again as well."

It had taken her a beat to make that admission, and Rory could almost see her face, flushed with embarrassment.

"I'm glad you missed me, sweetheart. I missed you, too." He didn't give himself time to think twice before asking, "Would you like to spend tomorrow evening with me? We have the day off. I could come and get you from work and we could have a lovely night in. What do you say?" *Please don't say no, love.*

"I'd like that, Rory."

His fist pump of glee was immensely satisfying. "Go back to sleep now, love. I'll call you tomorrow when I'm on the way, okay?"

"Okay. G'night, Rory."

"Night night, little kitten."

With nothing planned when he woke up, he went for his morning run and then made his way down to his kitchen to figure out what he wanted for breakfast. The lads would all stop by for lunch to finalize any changes they wanted to make for the final show, but he'd make sure they understood that his evening was taken. Sausages and eggs on toast sounded like a plan. He brewed tea while he got out the ingredients and sipped it while the meat and eggs cooked.

When everything was ready, he took his meal and a second cup of tea out to the back patio and listened to the morning birds sing at each other while he savored the flavors on his plate. Will called as he was finishing his tea.

"Morning, Ro. Are we still on for the lunch meeting?"

"Yes. What? Haven't had enough of wifey?"

"You may tease, but wait until it's your turn," Will warned him, chuckling. "Then *I'll* be the one laughing at *you*."

Rory chuckled with him. "I don't see an issue with any of that. I *wish* I had your problem, mate."

"Give her time, Ro. She'll come round." Will's tone was as warm as his words were encouraging.

"She'll be round this evening, so you'll need to help me get the lads off to the pub or wherever when I leave to get her from work."

"I've got your back, don't worry. We'll bring lunch so you won't have to worry about that. See you later. Oh, and Dawn says hi."

Rory heard Will's wife's voice in the background, and he sent her his own greetings before he hung up. His housekeeper had been in earlier in the week to get the house ready for his return, and he was pleased that he didn't have to do more than pick up after himself in the master suite and make his bed. What could he make Chrissy this time for dinner? Maybe he should take a leaf out of Will's book and order in. That was probably a better idea. He pulled all his favorite take-away menus out of the drawer in the kitchen island and looked them over, trying to decide which one he thought she would like.

This was the perfect excuse for calling her again, even though he knew she was at work and might not answer him. *Which would defeat the purpose of calling her, Ro, so why do it?* He sent her a text message instead.

[Rory: Do you prefer Indian or Thai food?]

Prepared to wait a few minutes since she was at work, he was surprised when his phone pinged almost instantly with her reply.

[Kitten: Either one is fine with me, thank you. I love them both.]

[Rory: Good to know. What time shall I come to get you?]

This time he waited five minutes before she responded.

[Kitten: Sorry I didn't answer sooner. The boss came in with more work. So maybe six this evening. If it'll be any earlier or any later, I'll send you a message.]

An hour later, he heard the lads coming down to where he was already in the studio, teasing out some lyrics for the new song he was composing. The song was for Chrissy, though he'd keep that to himself. For now. He loved his bandmates as if they were his brothers, but like brothers, they'd take the piss out of him if they knew how gone he was over her. Only Will knew the full extent of his feelings and that was more than enough for now.

"Morning all!"

"Been at it already, eh, Ro?" Will said. "How far along are you?"

"Not far enough. This can wait, though. We need to work on the latest one, if we're going to do it tomorrow night for the first time."

"We decided to order pizza for lunch," Tris informed him. He had designated himself the take-away guy, and all orders for delivery were made through him. He apparently had an app for every kind of restaurant or something ... Rory had no idea.

"Pizza's fine, just make sure there's at least half of one with nothing on it but bacon, thanks."

"I remember, Ro. And no one wants to share a pineapple and bacon one with me, right?"

Groans and insults flew back and forth for a minute while Rory just listened and smiled. He was glad he enjoyed his workmates' antics, otherwise he'd be a very unhappy camper. They were, by turns, the coolest, most grown-up, and most juvenile men he knew.

Henry clapped his hands together. "Alright now, time for work, lads. Can the silliness, and let's get down to it. We're beginning with 'Where The Love Is.' Warmups, then we'll do it."

After more than three hours of solid work, they stopped for a well-earned rest. Tris ordered their pizzas, and he let them help themselves to whatever they fancied drinking from the drink refrigerator. They'd worked up an appetite, especially once they got all the cues in that first ballad right. A couple of other energetic favorites that had John headbanging like the pro he was, and they were wiped. A good hour of rest, some good food, and laughter would serve them well.

"I have a date this evening," Rory announced.

Whoops and salacious commentary followed his announcement. He ignored the lot of them, even though he grinned as widely as they did. He couldn't disguise his joy if he tried, so he didn't bother.

"So you're all invited to push off around half four or so. Gives me enough time to clean up and go get her."

More typically lewd suggestions about what he might be doing on his date followed, and he flipped them all off as he finished his third slice of pizza. They had literally ordered half a pizza for him with only bacon. The other half had pineapple added for Tris.

"Saving the last slice for Chrissy, then?" Will asked, smirking.

"Belt up, you prat!"

Will was undeterred by the insult, and he didn't shut up, as he'd been invited to do. Instead, he opened his mouth, most likely to say something that would earn him a punch on the arm, when his phone rang.

"Saved by the bell," Rory quipped, and found himself on the receiving end of a two-fingered salute.

Once Will ended the call, they got back to work, and managed to finish everything they'd planned on doing by four. They all helped to set the room to rights before heading back upstairs for a last drink, men's room breaks, and reminders about the next day's agenda.

"Don't forget we have an early rehearsal tomorrow, Ro. No sleeping in."

That time, it was Henry doing the teasing, though he was also serious. Their London shows were always specially choreographed, and there was always a light show and pyrotechnics, which meant they'd need to be there sooner, and soundchecks would likely last longer than usual. And tomorrow night, there was to be a reception after the show to which a few select people had been invited to meet the band. Rory would make sure that he reserved a ticket for Chrissy. He didn't want to be without her then, not just because he wanted to hold onto her for as long as he could this weekend, but also because she'd be a deterrent to the sex-hungry groupies who were a constant in London.

The lads left by four thirty as he'd wished, and he went up to shower and change. Even though they'd be coming back to his place for dinner and a movie—and hopefully more—he wanted to look good for his woman. Stonewashed jeans, a royal blue distressed t-shirt, his black leather vest, and boots gave him the rockstar vibe without being outrageous, and he knew Chrissy would be comfortable around him dressed that way. He called her when he started the car.

"I'm on my way, love. Meet you in front in half an hour, yes?"

"Okay."

He hoped that the hoarseness that he detected in her voice was because she'd been dying to see him all day and was worked up now that he'd called to say he was on the way. He knew that *he* was worked up, and he did his best to calm himself before he got there. Humming the lyrics to an old band favorite, he managed to calm his cock down from half-mast, and then he saw her when he looked up from putting the car in park.

"Jesus!" He whispered the Lord's name aloud like a prayer for control as she turned to smile at the woman who had walked out with her before turning back to head his way. "Down boy!" he implored his once-again-rising dick, which almost gleefully ignored his plea and perked up more the closer she got. Adjusting himself as best he could, he got out and walked around to open her door for her.

Chrissy was wearing a pretty dark gray pant-suit under the jacket of which was a hot pink blouse. Her hair was swept up on top of her head, with a wisp or two falling down over her face. It didn't look like artifice, but rather like it had genuinely come loose from the topknot she had in place, and she had just given up on getting it back in order. It was sexy as sin, and her arched brows and full, red-painted lips made him groan louder as she approached.

"Hi," she said when she got to him. "Thanks for picking me up, though I'm never going to hear the end of it now."

He got her settled in the seat, then walked around to his side, and as he pulled out into traffic, he asked, "Hear the end of what, love?"

"That was Moira I was talking to just now. She had to work late as well, and is meeting her friend for drinks at the pub. But I know she's going to tell the others."

"Tell them...?" Rory thought he knew, but he wanted her to confirm his suspicions.

"That you were the one picking me up. She asked me how I was getting home earlier when we knew we had to do a bit of overtime, and I said a friend was coming to get me." She sighed heavily, a very put-upon sigh. "Then she saw you get out of the car, and she got really excited, asked me if you were really who she thought you were, and was about to start a whole conversation, but I told her I'd fill her in on Monday."

"Does it bother you that she knows who your friend is? You didn't claim me as your boyfriend, so what's the big deal?" He refused to feel disappointed.

"I'm not cool enough to be friends with a rockstar, Rory!" she snapped, then immediately apologized. "It's not your fault that I'm socially awkward."

Rory reached for her hand and pulled it over to the console, keeping his own over it as he drove.

"Maybe it won't be so bad," he remarked. "After all, they're friendly, aren't they, even if they're not exactly your friends."

He knew how meticulous she was about relationships, not wanting to claim more than she thought existed between her and others. Hence, this conversation about what to call him. He would be patient, especially since he planned to become more than just her boyfriend anyway.

CHAPTER 11

C hrissy held herself as still as a stone in the quiet pool of the car, not moving even when Rory held her hand on the console between their seats. He didn't seem to be especially concerned about being seen with her, so why was she stressing over it? Maybe he just didn't understand how vastly different their lives were. Sure, he knew how she'd been raised by nuns. He knew she had lived a very sheltered life. And now he even knew she was a virgin. So far, he hadn't balked at the idea of being with her, but he hadn't spent more than a couple of hours with her at a time, and that wasn't conducive to getting to know someone.

She let herself hope that her fears were groundless, that Rory wanted more from her than to get into her knickers. She wasn't naive enough to think he didn't want that. She'd seen how his eyes roamed over her, filled with a heat that she could only assume was lust and hunger. It was a boost to her ego to know that she was the object of his desire. But who could say how long that would last, especially if she never let him get past the kissing stage?

"What are you thinking so hard about over there, hmm?"

Oh no! There was no way in hell she was ever sharing all the thoughts that had just passed through her mind.

"Nothing really," she hedged. "Just letting my mind wander."

"Should I be offended that you're not thinking about me? About what kind of mischief we might get into tonight?"

She knew he was teasing her, and she loved it, but it also made her very self-conscious because she had been thinking about the way he looked at her as if he wouldn't mind enjoying her. What would that look like? Feel like? How did her skin feel to him? Did he love her curves? Did he mind that there were a lot of them?

She'd learned to deflect attention from herself from an early age by appearing to exude a confidence she was far from feeling. That usually came out as words designed to fool people into thinking she had herself together. She tried that tactic again.

"I didn't know that agreeing to dinner meant I was signing up for mischief. I should be the one offended, shouldn't I, since you left out vital information when you issued the invitation."

There, that should do it. Enough to keep him from focusing on what she'd been thinking so hard about. That was all she wanted.

Rory laughed. It was a light and cheerful sound, making her chest warm and her toes curl. Who knew a laugh could have such a physical impact on a person? When he had control of himself, he squeezed her hand and pulled it further over so it was resting on his thigh. The warmth of his flesh beneath his jeans was a brand on her palm, and she could not escape as he held her hand there, relentless in his need for contact.

"You're a bundle of contradictions, did you know that? And in case you haven't figured it out as yet, I find that sexy as hell." He raised her hand to his lips and kissed the knuckles before returning it to his thigh. "So even though you're dead set against telling me what had you so quiet earlier, I have my ways to get you to talk, little kitten. And your attempt at distraction just gave me permission to use whichever of them I wish to on you."

Chrissy had no response for that, so she said nothing, which seemed to amuse Rory even more. She didn't like being the butt of his joke, but she'd been the one to start it with her refusal to share what she was thinking. Maybe if she tried to share some part of it, he'd be less amused? If she could just let go, everything would be easier, she was sure of it. She could flirt with Rory and not be so super aware of who he was if she would just relax.

When pigs fly, her unbelieving inner voice whispered in her head. She shushed it, needing to believe anything was possible if she set her mind to it. She had started on this new path because she wanted to grow, and she'd accepted the invitation to his home because she knew that she wanted more than a few kisses. There was no shame in admitting it, if only to herself.

"We'll stop to get the takeaway, then go home. Would you like anything else while we're out?"

"No, I'm fine, thank you."

Once he'd picked up the food—and Chrissy shook her head in amazement at the number of bags he brought back to the car with him—they got back to his home in less than twenty minutes. She helped him with the bags and watched as he sorted the things he had ordered and set the boxes on the table.

"Shall I lay the table for you?" She needed to help instead of standing there like a helpless fool.

"That would be lovely, thank you. Utensils are in the top drawer to the left of the stove." He indicated where they were and then added, "Let's eat in here."

She could see the plates and glasses through the glass cupboard doors, and once she was done setting places for two on the wide kitchen table, he pulled out a chair for her.

"Thank you."

She sat primly, waiting for him to take his seat and admiring the beautiful glass placemats sitting above a pretty sky-blue tablecloth. Each mat had a scene from a different city in England, recognizable by the landmarks displayed on them.

"These are lovely," she told him as he poured her a drink. "Did you buy them yourself?"

He smiled but didn't respond to her question immediately. "Help yourself to whatever you'd like. I've got biryani, naan, rogan josh, tandoori chicken, and vindaloo. I thought we could try some new dishes together, and I know you don't mind if it's a little spicier than usual. And there's ice cream for after, to cool the heat if you choose the vindaloo."

Chrissy gawked at him. "Rory, we can't possibly eat all this."

"We can always have the rest tomorrow, love."

What? His nonchalant response sent her nerves ticking over again like a wind-up toy. Was he suggesting that she...? No, he couldn't possibly be saying what she was thinking. That was just impossible. Best not to even entertain the thought.

Move on, Christina! She looked around, trying to find something else to focus on, anything other than his words. "And where are the samosas? Surely you didn't get Indian food and not order those?"

He stood up at once, saying as he crossed back to the bags, "Thanks. I forgot them. I bought lamb ones, because I'm a serious carnivore, in case you hadn't noticed."

He brought the samosas over to the table and sat again, reaching for one and saying, "So is that a yes or a no to spending the night with me?"

She almost choked on the piece of naan that she'd just swallowed. Taking a sip of her drink to clear her throat, she looked into his eyes, seeing heat and amusement there. So she hadn't been wrong after all. How had she not thought he might want this? She wasn't prepared to spend the night. And what if he meant for her to spend *more* than a night?

"Oh, and while you're thinking on that, what about spending the whole weekend with me? I have a VIP pass for you for tomorrow night's concert, and I'd love it if you came home with me after the show."

Chrissy's eyes had widened as he spoke, and now she had apparently gone speechless. The simple answer, of course, would be, "No, I can't spend the weekend with you. I have no clothes here." But her life hadn't been simple since she'd met Rory a year ago, and she might just be beginning to feel a thread of anticipation for the next adventure with him. Spending the night or the weekend would definitely qualify as an adventure for her safety-first soul.

"I don't have anything to wear." Every woman's excuse, only this was a fact of her life.

"I can either drop you at a dress shop to get something pretty, or I can take you home to choose from your wardrobe." He bit into the samosa he had picked up when he dropped the first bombshell question. "So yes or no, love? Will you stay with me this weekend?"

Her head gave the assent before she found her voice to say the word, which Rory waited patiently to hear. What had she just done? She stuffed half a samosa into her mouth as though it could erase her consent and pull her back from the edge she'd just gone over. She had never done anything this impulsive or this daring in her whole life. Not even her move to London had been bold. It had taken her almost a year of thinking and planning and researching before she finally said goodbye to the only home she had ever known.

"I can almost feel you panicking, Chrissy," Rory commented, finishing his samosa and helping himself to some of the vindaloo. "I promise that nothing will happen that you don't consent to. I give you my word, love." He pressed a hand to his heart before adding, "Now come on, eat up before the food gets cold."

Channeling her inner marionette, she nodded again and put food on her plate, not really noticing what she chose. She ate slowly, enjoying the flavors but not paying too much attention to what she put in her mouth. Her focus was more on Rory, who cleared his plate in record time and took seconds, choosing different food this time. He must be really hungry.

He caught her looking and grinned. "Your belly won't get full by watching me eat, little kitten," he teased.

She blushed and managed to finish eating without making a further fool of herself. When she wiped her lips on the napkin beside her plate, he said, "Ready for some ice cream?"

"That would be nice, thank you." Anything to cool her feverish thoughts as well as her tongue.

"Let's clear up this mess first, and then we can sit in the lounge."

Chrissy was all for staying busy. She definitely didn't want to think about what was going to happen after they left the kitchen. Whether they were just going to watch television as they ate their ice cream or get more comfortable and ... She bumped into a hard chest and realized that she'd not been paying attention to where she was going.

"Oh! Sorry!" She tried to step around him, but Rory held her by her upper arms.

"You're still panicking, love. What can I do to calm your nerves, hmm?" He tilted her chin so he could see her eyes. "Look at me, little kitten. I need to see these eyes of yours."

When she didn't comply, keeping her lashes low, he sighed heavily and dropped a swift, searing kiss on her lips. Still not releasing her chin, he repeated his request.

"Eyes on me, love. We have to work on your stress relief."

Did he really think her stress would be relieved by looking him in the eye? She snorted disbelievingly.

"What was that? I don't think you believe in my skills. I see I'll have to prove it to you."

Lowering his head, he claimed her mouth again, pulling her fully into his embrace and commandeering her lips and tongue, kissing her like his life depended on it, like their survival was not guaranteed without it. Chrissy didn't realize she'd wrapped her own arms around him until he lifted his head and whispered, "Have I restored your faith in my abilities now, sweet one?"

She had no idea what he was saying. Her brain was still befuddled by the kiss that she hadn't wanted to end and by thoughts of how she could get back the press of his lips and the heat of his tongue in her mouth. Maybe if she raised up on tiptoe? Suiting action to words, she lifted up and closed her eyes like a baby bird seeking food.

"Oh love, do you need another kiss? Where do you want it?" he mused. "Here?" He dropped a teasing peck on her forehead. When she didn't respond except to whine faintly, he continued. "No? Not there? How about here?" Another quick press of closed lips on her left cheek. "Or here?" Then her right. Then he slid his hands down to her bottom and pulled her forcefully into his body. There was no chance of her missing the huge erection that he was pressing into her belly.

She growled—actually growled, for heaven's sake!—needing the teasing to cease and the kissing to recommence. Rory chuckled softly at her, smoothing his thumbs over her cheekbones and down to her slightly parted lips. She wasn't getting enough oxygen from breathing through her nose, so panting seemed the best option she had if she were to remain upright.

"Did you just growl at me, my little lioness?"

He didn't seem nearly as surprised as she'd been at the sound of frustration that had escaped her. And she didn't like that he found it amusing either. She had never been as turned on as she was, never felt quite so wound up and out of control, as though a hot wind would engulf her in unquenchable flames. And all he'd done was kiss her. The need still rising inside her like lava about to erupt sent words shooting from her mouth that she had had no intention of speaking.

"Please, Rory, I need..."

Now it was his turn to growl, only this was no sound of frustration. It was possessive and hungry.

"What do you need, love? Tell me."

In for a penny, in for a pound, as they say. "I need your mouth on mine again, please." At least she could be polite about it, even if her dampening panties said she had the right to make demands.

Another growl, louder, fiercer, while his hands tightened on her arse cheeks and he ground himself harder against her. They swayed where they stood in the middle of the kitchen floor, while Rory gave her what she'd ordered. Kiss after ravenous kiss, plumbing the recesses of her mouth, feasting on her tongue and lips, plunging in and out in imitation of what she was sure was a different, more intimate kind of penetration, made her tremble like a sapling in a gale. When he finally released her mouth, she was gasping for air, weak, wanting more, craving things she wasn't sure she understood, knowing only that whatever she wanted, Rory could supply it.

"Come on," he said, pulling her along with him to the lounge and down over his lap to straddle him in the recliner, before he started in on the kissing again.

Now, with her legs spread wide, she could feel his knob as it jerked beneath her, and he pulled on her hips to get her to ride him. They were both still fully clothed, and Chrissy was feeling warmer by the second. She'd discovered her clitoris when she hit puberty and she knew the pleasure it could give if she rubbed it right. But this, with Rory, was next-level satisfaction, and they were just humping each other through their clothes.

"I need to touch you, sweetheart," Rory said, as if he had read her mind. "But only if you want me to."

Her brain stuttered on the idea. If her fingers brought her such delight, what would it be like when an experienced man with big fingers played with her? The thought of Rory's fingers diddling her hot button made her body clench. She moaned helplessly, feeling at once impossibly aroused and overwhelmingly embarrassed at her over-the-top response to just his words.

Rory leaned in. "Nod for yes, love," he whispered, nipping her earlobe and scraping his teeth down the side of her neck before searching out her lips again.

Somewhere in the far corners of her lust-drunk brain, amusement flared at the assumption that his last words made. What if she wanted to say no? But even as she thought it, she knew she would be lying if she even pretended that she didn't want whatever he wanted to do to her. He had her full consent to debauch her completely if he so chose.

She nodded when he released her lips, and he groaned and pushed at her jacket. She helped him to remove it, then raised her arms so he could pull the pink blouse over her head. His hands found her full breasts, encased in practical black cotton bra with a whimsical lace trim above each cup and down the sides. Would he find her choice of unsophisticated undergarments a turnoff? Did he prefer lace and silk and satin on his women? How did she measure up under her clothes?

"I appreciate the front closure of this bra more than you will ever know."

His voice saying those ridiculous words drew her attention back to the man unhooking the bra's clasps and pushing the straps down her arms.

"Mmff!" He buried his face between her breasts and groaned, kneading them like dough. "You're so soft, sweetheart. Mmm!"

He lowered his mouth to lick one nipple while squeezing the other between his fingers, all without taking his eyes off hers. And she was too mesmerized by the darkening blue gaze that held her captive to do more than gaze back at him and gasp out the pleasure he was giving her just from fondling and licking her breasts. Who knew her nipples were an erogenous zone? She certainly knew now.

"Oh gosh, that feels ... mmm, oh..." Nonsense was spewing from her lips without conscious thought. "Oh, goodness, Rory!" She bit her lip, trying to stem the flow of words, but he kept up the assault on her senses, making it impossible to stay silent. "Please, it's so ... unh! Oh, so good!" She threw her head back and shut her eyes then, unable to hold his fiery gaze any longer.

"Mmmmmm!" Rory's response was a long purr of approval. "Can I make you come like this, sweetheart?"

He probably could, she thought, the idea of it sending a fresh spurt of juice into her dampening undies. He switched sides, adding teeth to the mix of sensual torture, using them to scrape the tender flesh of her breasts and to leave butterfly nips on her dusky flesh. She gasped as sensations flashed through her, settling in her core, and her inner muscles tightened in anticipation of more.

Which reminded her, she might as well keep speaking up for herself. "Please, Rory, please!"

He released her nipple with a pop and pulled her so close that his t-shirt took over the task of keeping her sensitized to his every touch. Her belly clenched when he kissed her again, this time sliding his hand down the front placket of her slacks.

"Please, Rory," she pleaded.

"Tell me what you want, sweetheart."

He nipped her bottom lip, pulling it away from her teeth. Chrissy followed his mouth blindly when he let her go, seeking another kiss.

"Uh uh! You have a request to finish," he said, shaking his head at her attempt. "I need to hear the words, love. Tell me what you need from me."

"Touch me," she groaned, undone and unable to hold back her need a second more.

"Where?"

Was he trying to drive her mad? Her eyes slammed open, and she glared at him, hungry and demanding.

"Don't tease me!" She wanted to sound annoyed, but all she heard was desperation.

"My poor little kitten," he murmured, undoing the clasp at her waist and pulling down the zipper. "Stand up, love. We need to get these off, don't we?"

Her bra fell to the floor as she stood up from his lap but before he could strip her naked, she was on him, suddenly unafraid to take what she wanted. And what she wanted at the moment was to see his naked chest, to trail her fingers through the hair on it and down his abs, to see what that bulge in his jeans looked like without the screen of clothing. She needed to touch him in the same way that he'd been touching her.

Where had this boldness come from? She didn't know, and she couldn't care just at the moment as she unbuckled his belt and unbuttoned the fly of his jeans. She was doing this. It was time.

CHAPTER 12

Chrissy's hands were trembling as she unbuttoned Rory's fly. He felt every touch and every breath. He swore he could almost hear the rapid beating of her heart as she undressed him. Not that his own heartbeat was any more sedate. In fact, his was racing from an overload of lust and need and anticipation as he'd seduced her with his lips, his tongue, his fingers, his words. He'd teased her mercilessly, knowing how it would push her to a fever pitch of desire and leave her open to anything he wanted.

So now that he had driven her insane with lust, he was forced to endure her awkward ministrations as she took his clothes off him. He wanted to give her back a little of the control he had stripped from her with his kisses and caresses, just enough that she would know how very much he was in the same boat as she was. If she knew how she made him ache and burn and tremble with desire for her, it would make it easier for her to give in to his demands when he chose to make them.

He hadn't meant to go this far just yet. Some heavy petting had been the planned next step with his little kitten, but she had wrenched control from him when she'd begged him to touch her, and there was nothing he could have done aside from give in to what she needed. He had heard the almost desperate tone of her last plea for him not to tease her. He hissed as her hands trailed down his belly, and she gripped the silky hairs on his chest and pulled gently.

Bloody hell! She was going to drive him as mad with desire as he'd been doing her. He loved having his hair played with, whether on his head or on his body.

"Darling, now you're teasing me," he whispered, giving her the truth even as he settled his lips over hers for a softer, more tender kiss.

She turned startled eyes up to his as if she were shocked at his admission. How could she not know what she did to him? He smiled at her as she tore her gaze away to push his jeans down his legs. Unsurprisingly, she left his boxers where they were. He'd let her get away with it this time. They were supposed to be going slow, after all, so keeping their lower bodies semi-clothed was permissible, even advisable. He kicked off the jeans, saying as he did so, "Take your slacks off, love, and then come sit on me again."

The plain black bikini panties with the lace trim that she wore matched her bra in every detail, including the fact that the front placket was made entirely of lace, so he could catch glimpses of her mound covered in hair. He itched to slide his hands beneath the waistband, to feel the hairs it hid. Would they be springy and tickle his palm, or would they be smooth and velvety? The feel of her warm center covering his cock pulled him from his daze.

"Mmm. You're so warm, sweetheart."

He thrust up against her and held her hips, so she had no choice but to take the pressure of his heavy erection against her folds. Her answering press down on his hardness dragged a satisfied groan from his throat. He did it again, and she imitated his action, letting a moan of pleasure escape her.

"You like that, love? You like me pressing in on your sweet button like that?"

She nodded and swallowed, letting out her breath in a soft pant against his lips. He took them, suckling and stroking them with his tongue before he settled his mouth over hers and mimicked the action of his hips. Kissing her was like nothing he'd ever experienced before. He could feel her innocence and the fire that lit her up and sent her tongue out to meet his in a frenzy of desire.

There was no artifice in her kisses, only pure want and need and the desire to give him back everything that he was giving her. When she wrapped her arms around his neck and pressed down harder against him, he groaned and pulled his mouth away to ask, "Do you want more, baby?"

She raised lust-laden eyes to his own, lingering on his mouth a long moment before holding his gaze and nodding. And then she gave him the words, as though she remembered how he always asked her to speak her need.

"Yes, I want more, please."

Still so damned polite, it shook him to the marrow of his bones, and his cock jerked against her in response. How did such a simple word have such a profound effect on him? It never had before, not in all the hookups he'd had over the years. But this sweet, hot little woman now squirming on his lap, begging with her gyrating hips for him to give her more, could make him as hard as stone with just that one plea.

"It'll feel even better if we're skin to skin, love," he murmured, hissing when she pressed harder against him. Fuck! He shivered as he waited for her to decide, feeling hot and cold at the same time from the excess of emotion that swept over him.

"Okay."

Another single word with the power to unman him. He eased up with her still straddling him and pulled his boxers down until his cock was exposed. Then he reached down, fighting to keep his hand steady, and pulled aside the very damp seat of her panties. Hissing at the heat radiating off her wet lips, he slid a finger up to find her clitoris fully extended and pulsing.

"Oh, fuck, baby, you're so wet for me!"

He was panting now, sliding his finger up and down between her lips, not penetrating her, just playing with her little love button and reveling in the repeated gasps of pleasure that seemed to be emanating from the bottom of her soul. She was on fire, and when he finally slid the tip of a finger into her soaking hole, she gasped and bore down on him, taking him in all the way.

"Jesus, Mary, and Joseph!" she whisper-screamed, hiding her face in his neck but still riding his finger.

"What would your sainted aunties say if they heard you taking the Lord's name in vain, little kitten?"

He needed to tease her, to help her keep control. He didn't want her cumming just yet. He wanted to discover all her erotic buttons, so he could push them and edge her until she couldn't take another touch without falling over the edge. She ignored his comment, only driving her hips up and down on his finger. And when he inserted a second, she cried out and sat down on him, taking them all the way into her body.

God, he was done for! He needed his hard cock inside her yesterday or he was sure he'd expire. She lifted her hips, and he went back to cradling them in his hands while she hovered over his uncovered dick. Just as she was descending, no doubt to swallow him whole with her ready body, his brain came back online.

"Shit! Condoms, darling. We need condoms."

She gasped and hid her face in the crook of his neck. She was trembling hard now, her need and her fear beating against him like living things. He was damned if he was going to move now. He'd find another way to get them off without losing touch with her.

"Here, this is what we'll do, love."

Turning, he lay back on the recliner, pushed his boxers all the way off, and settled her above him. Then, letting his cock remain where it lay against his belly, he pulled her up by the hips and said, "You can ride me like this, sweetheart."

He pulled her hips forward until her lips engulfed his dick, then slid her backwards off them. He helped her to do it a few more times, and then he let go of her hips because she was a fast learner, and in no time, she was teasing the head of his dick and sliding her juicy center along its length while he played with her nipples. The sounds they were making would make any porn star jealous and keep the show's producer happy beyond words as they humped each other.

"Feel good, baby?" he asked, panting between thrusts. "Want me to make you come?"

"Yes, oh, Jesus, yes!"

Her answering cry shot spunk into his balls, and he slid his fingers back in, determined not to come before she took her pleasure. He found the bundle of nerves inside that made her scream his name, her hips jerking spasmodically as she came in waves. Keeping his fingers inside her, he enclosed her hand in his and wrapped them both around his cock, pumping it hard. Then he let go and let her finish him, cumming in jets of semen over her hand and up his belly.

Somewhere in the recesses of his brain, where sex had not completely scrambled his thinking processes, he felt pride in the way she pumped him until his cock stopped jerking in orgasm. And as his body slowed, she slowed her movements until she was gently stroking him, as though she was reluctant to release him.

They came down slowly, Chrissy's face mashed into the curve of his neck, her fingers just holding his softening dick, his still buried inside her. He wiggled them and she gasped, making him smile.

"I love how you came for me, little kitten," he whispered in her ear. "You're so sexy when you scream my name." He felt her smile against his neck and pulled her head up so they could look into each other's eyes. "Are you okay?" He searched her face for his answer, but she kept her eyes lowered. "Look at me, sweetheart, please."

Now *he* was begging, but he didn't care. He needed to know that it had been as good for her as it had been for him. He tilted her chin up, and finally, she let him see her eyes. They were swimming in tears. Shit! Had he hurt her?

"Chrissy, please tell me if I've hurt you, love."

She shook her head. "You didn't hurt me." She smiled, a rainbow in the rain. "These aren't sad tears."

He couldn't help it then. He kissed her, taking charge of her lips and tongue, deepening it until his cock began to stir again. She must have felt it because she looked down at it, shock and delight in her eyes. He chuckled, unable to keep his amusement to himself.

"Yes," he murmured. "We can do it again as soon as I've had a bit of a rest, okay?" He nipped the tip of her nose. "Would you like that?"

She hesitated and his heartbeat sputtered. Was she going to send him packing now, after what they'd just done together? Had he really gone too far after all?

"I would like that and more," she declared resolutely, and then bit back a yawn.

"Come on, let's get you cleaned up and into bed. Hold on to me."

Standing with her, he made his way up to the foot of the stairs and then slid her down his body, letting her stand on her own before leading her up the stairs to his bathroom. He set the water for the shower and pulled her under it the minute it was warm enough. She hadn't said a word since they'd left the lounge, and he could see the pull of sleep on her eyelids. Was she one of those people who got knocked out after good sex? How would it be when he took her completely?

The thought of his cock buried in her heat was enough to move it from flagging to half-mast. He ignored it, washing her and setting her on her feet completely so she could step out and dry herself off.

"Go wait for me, love," he told her. "I'll be right with you."

She was asleep when he got back into the bedroom, her body slack and lush against his cream-colored sheets. He tucked her in on her side, climbed in next to her, and big-spooned her, pulling the covers over both of them. She was soft and warm against his chest, down his thighs, and under his arm and hand. He kissed the shell of her ear, whispering, "Sleep sweet, darling."

CHAPTER 13

When Rory woke up, Chrissy was gone, and his bed was cold. *Bollocks! Where the hell was she?* Scrambling out of bed, he hurried to empty his bladder, which was screaming at him for relief, washed his hands, and pulled on his boxers and robe before going in search of his love. She'd better not have left, or he'd be royally pissed off. It was just past eight in the morning, and he found her curled up on the sofa, snuggled under a blanket fast asleep.

What had made her leave his bed and the comfort of his arms to sleep alone in a cold front room? If she'd been uncomfortable, why hadn't she just gone to sleep in one of the guest rooms? He walked over to her, careful to step as soundlessly as possible, and saw the photo album she'd left lying on the floor next to her.

A smile broke over his face. He understood curiosity. He understood wanting to know more about an unknown entity, like he was to her, in order to become more familiar with it before committing to anything long-term. Last night's lovemaking had been a fluke, born of an excess of ardor built up over a long and aching period of time. But the next time, it would be born of a complete understanding not just of their over-whelming need for each other, but of their full consent to give and take as equal partners in passion.

Should he wake her up and take her back to bed? His heart and his body were on board with the yes that swelled in him, but his mind said he'd be better off letting her wake on her own and sleep where she was most comfortable. Knowing *he* wouldn't go back to sleep, he went into the kitchen to brew himself some tea and made a pot of coffee as well, in case she preferred that in the morning.

Whatever it was that woke her, when he walked back into the living room, prepared to sit across from her and watch her sleep, she was awake and sitting up, yawning hugely. He stepped into her field of vision, and her eyes snapped to his immediately.

"Good morning, little kitten. Did you sleep well?"

He wouldn't ask about why she hadn't ended her night in his arms. She was probably going to beat herself up about that, anyway, worrying if she had hurt his feelings or might seem ungrateful. He wouldn't add to her stress. Mornings were meant for lazy reflection, for thankfulness, for love-making. Two out of three ain't bad, like the song said, right? When she gave a low "Yes, thank you" in answer to his question, he continued, "Would you like some tea? Coffee?"

"Tea, please, just honey."

She swung her legs out from under the blanket, throwing it off before swinging them down to the floor, and Rory got a glimpse of a lush thigh and one round cheek of her bare arse. His cock hardened instantly. She stood up, in his t-shirt and nothing more, and he had to shove his unoccupied hand deep into the pocket of his robe to stop himself from reaching for her as she walked by him.

"Need the loo," she whispered, face flushed.

"No rush. I'll bring it upstairs, love."

He turned and walked away before she could respond. He didn't want to talk about why he wanted her back in his room, hopefully at least sitting on the edge of his big bed. He just knew he needed to see her in his private space again, to inhale her fragrance while she was still his, before he had to take her home to prepare for their date later at the concert. Maybe, if he was lucky, he could get her off at least once more before they had to push off. The lads were expecting him at the facility by eleven, so he'd need to take her home before then.

He carried her teacup to her and found her setting her clothes out on the bed, preparing to get dressed.

"Here, let's sit in the alcove and drink our tea. We've got a couple of hours before we have to leave."

He led the way to the bay window and sat down, turning to her as she joined him and handing her the teacup in its saucer. He took a sip of his own brew and grinned when she asked, "Why didn't I get a mug as well?"

She was eyeing his Dr. Who mug almost enviously. He chuckled. "I thought you'd like a delicate china teacup," he said. "Besides, they'd never get used if I didn't offer them to my guests."

She pursed her lips, humming at him disbelievingly. "So your bandmates get the teacups as well?"

He laughed outright at her attempt to catch him off guard. "They're not guests. They're mates. Each of them has his own mug here anyway, and they'd laugh me out of my house if I tried to offer them a teacup." He tilted his head as an idea formed, and he spoke it before he could overthink it. "Would you like to choose a mug for yourself? That way, I'll know what to give you your tea in the next time you're over."

Not subtle, but he wasn't trying to be slick this early in the morning. Anything to get her back in his space was worth a try, even cheesy lines about mugs.

"Such a tempting offer," she replied drily, obviously trying not to laugh. "How can I possibly say no?"

He smiled but didn't reply. That had sounded like a yes to him. They'd choose her mug when they went back downstairs for breakfast. Now he turned to look out the window at the early morning brightness of his backyard. Sunlight dappled the water in the pool with the shadows from the trees that stood near it. The colors of the flowers were intensified by the light ... or maybe that was just his mood making him see things that were no different today than they'd been yesterday.

"Do you ever have breakfast down there?" she asked, looking down at the outdoor sitting area.

"Sometimes, yes, when I'm not in a hurry to be anywhere. Why? Would you like to eat outside today?"

Her eyes were sparkling pools of quiet happiness as she nodded and sipped her tea. "I'd like to hear the birds."

The way she bit her lip, a small smile curving them, the way she licked them when a drop of tea lingered, the way her eyes lit up as she watched the birds in the birdbath all kept his body at full attention. He was glad he could keep the hand holding the mug in his lap. He could hide his hardening erection much better that way without drawing attention to his predicament.

By contrast, she seemed entirely too serene and unmoved by the situation, until she caught him watching her and the hand holding her teacup trembled ever so slightly. Had he not been looking at her, he would have missed it. *That's right, sweetheart, feel it with me!* The sweet tension rising between them, fueled by nothing more than their nearness to each other, was powerfully arousing.

Putting his mug down on the floor, he leaned in. "May I borrow this?"

He held the saucer and she let it go. Placing it on the ground next to his mug, he reached for her, dragging her over to sit so close her knees rode over his, and then he took her lips. He needed her like bees needed nectar, like flowers needed sunshine, like rivers needed rain. Her mouth was soft and welcoming, and she tasted of the sweet dark tea she'd been drinking, full-bodied and mellow, like her breasts and her hips and the bounteous arse and strong arms that she wrapped around his neck as she pulled herself close enough to almost straddle his lap.

He moved, settling them so she could sit more comfortably atop his thighs, so her naked sheath could more easily accept the gift of his cock when he slid it between her hopefully wet folds. Needing to touch her there, to make sure she'd be ready for that less innocent touch, he slid a hand down to the tail of his t-shirt and slipped it beneath to search out her heat. He was rewarded with a gush of her essence when he slid his finger deep inside and pulled out her juices to slicken the lips of her sex and her clitoris.

"Ror..." she gasped, unable to even complete his name as he continued to fondle her.

"Love how you say my name, sweetheart. I want you to come for me again before we have to go."

"Mmm ... yes," she hummed, squirming as he teased her hungry flesh. "Oh please, yes."

Her innocent and heartfelt need echoed his own desire for her and sent his heart rate soaring. Pulling her up from the window seat and back to his bed, he laid her out like a feast, pulling the t-shirt off her body and stripping himself. Before he lay back and positioned himself so she could straddle him again, he feasted on her, taking all that her body gave him willingly, savoring the flavor of her desire.

"You're so sweet," he told her, sliding his tongue between her folds and lapping at her very erect love button.

Her gasps of pleasure were a melody he would never tire of hearing. Pulling her over onto his thighs, he spread the lips of her sex and slid his cock between them, thrusting as though he were penetrating her core, but only teasing her clitoris and soaking his shaft in her essence.

"Hold me, love, and ride me like this."

When she reached down to position his cock where it would have the maximum impact as she slid her bottom back and forth along his thighs, he hissed and grabbed her, helping her to slide over him. The touches weren't enough to get him off, but they kept him on the edge, especially when the head of his dick hitched at her entrance before sliding the rest of the way up to her clitoris.

"You like this, love?" he asked when a particularly hard thrust hit her just so and brought a long moan from her.

A groan was his only answer. Releasing her, he leaned up on his elbows for a moment to watch his cock slide between the lips of her sex, the sounds that their flesh made against each other as they played, adding to the symphony that her sighs and moans had begun. He looked up at her, head thrown back, eyes closed, mouth open to catch gulps of air, and his body tightened. He had to get inside her.

"Fuck, sweetheart, I need you."

He gave her the truth, pulling her flat and rolling with her so she was under him. Kissing her hard, he reared up from the bed and slid over to pull a condom from his nightstand. When he came back over her, he dropped the little silver packet on her belly and looked down at her, the question on the tip of his tongue. She didn't let him speak.

"Yes, please, Rory. Please!"

Thank fuck! "I won't hurt you, love, I promise, but I need to get you ready for me, okay?" She nodded, and the trust he saw shining in her eyes melted his bones and hardened his dick even more as he rolled on the protection.

She was so wet, he had no trouble sliding into her core, sending his finger up, searching for her g-spot and reveling in the cries that she couldn't hold in each time he hit it. Three fingers in and he was leaking like a sieve. His need for her rose like a head of foam, bubbling and fizzing, pushing him to take her hard. But she was a virgin, and he would be patient, take his time with her, so her pleasure would be absolute when he slid inside her.

"Are you ready for me, love?" he leaned in to ask against her lips.

She mewled and nodded, and he kissed her harder, ramming his cock head against her clitoris over and over, needing her to come one more time before he entered her pristine channel. The thought of her walls holding him in, squeezing him, pulling his seed from him, sent a fresh spurt of precum pushing from his slit. As though she had read his mind, she wailed as her orgasm overtook her, and Rory rode it out with her, lifting his hips away from her, breathing slowly to calm himself.

Then he settled his head against her folds and slid in, doing his best to make sure that, with his achingly slow movement, she would be as comfortable as possible when he pushed past any resistance. He knew when he moved past the evidence of her virginity because she gasped, and tears pooled in her eyes. But she never took them off him, and as he slid all the way in, her body relaxed, settling against him until, when he pulled out to push in again, she tried to hold on to him with the tight, strong walls of her core.

"I'm not leaving you, love," he promised, chuckling despite the intense emotions passing between them.

"Rory, please," she begged him when he slid back in.

He knew what she wanted, what they both needed, and he gave in to the irresistible urge to rut. Raising her legs to his shoulders, he plowed into her over and over, changing the angle of his hips when he found her g-spot and hitting it on every stroke, lifting them both higher and higher.

"Oh my god!" she screamed as she came again, harder than before, a long, powerful swell of pleasure that tightened her walls around him and dragged his seed from him in demanding contractions of her core along his length.

"Chrissyyyyy!"

He cried out her name, releasing her legs and settling his chest against her, belly to belly, leaving no space between them while he kept ramming her until his balls were empty. Gasping, he relaxed, feeling her heavy breaths matching his own as they fought for air. He'd never been with anyone like her before, so responsive to his touch, to the heat between them, her body molding to his and answering his lust with her own.

He smiled as he rolled off her, watching her doze. He had worn her out, but he couldn't feel bad about it. He loved it when a plan came together. The thought seemed familiar, like he'd heard the words somewhere before. Wherever he'd heard them, they were no less than the truth.

CHAPTER 14

"Calm down, Chrissy!" Toni's voice in her ear sounded a lot amused and a little exasperated. "Didn't you tell me you've already been to one of his concerts as a VIP guest?"

"Yes. So?"

What was the point of the question? And more to the point, how was it helping her to decide what to wear in—she glanced at the digital clock on her bedside table—in four hours?

Toni sighed. "Please know that I am officially rolling my eyes at you, which is not a good look on a thirty-seven-year-old woman. Chrissy, you already know exactly what to wear, so that's not the issue, is it?"

Of course, as usual, Toni was right. Chrissy supposed that that was why she was so good at her job. She was a past master—or should she say mistress?—at finding the root cause of the issues her clients faced ... well, were afraid to face, to be honest. Like she was now afraid to face her real concern, which was whether or not she was ready to step back onto the stage she'd run silently screaming from seven months ago.

Rory was still Riordan, rockstar extraordinaire. He was still the same talented, sexy man he'd been then. He still had a large and sometimes obsessive fan club, with groupies who exemplified the full meaning of the word fan. Could she go back to watching them throw themselves at him? Could she bear to stand by while the ones who got close fawned all over him as he signed autographs and posed for pictures? And could she bear to have the spotlight turned on her?

"Chrissy? Talk to me, sweetie. I can't help you if I don't have all the facts."

She'd called Toni as soon as Rory had dropped her off with a toe-curling kiss and a reminder to be ready by six when the limo would be there to pick her up. She'd been in panic mode, literally shaking with nerves, not only over what was to happen in the evening but also over what had happened the night before and earlier in the morning. She wasn't surprised that Toni figured something was up.

Chrissy had never called her on the weekend before, which, now that she was thinking about it was a really shitty thing to do to someone she called a friend. Toni had always been the one to do the calling and the inviting out. And the first time Chrissy was calling her, it was to ask for help because she was a panicking mess. She'd have to remedy that ASAP ... but not now. Now it was time for triage, or whatever they called it, when someone had to save her arse before she lit it on fire.

Heaving a sigh of her own, she gave the precise version of the last twelve hours.

"I had dinner with Rory and spent the night at his place."

Even though she was secretly thrilled that she'd finally given up her V-card—*Thank you, cheesy romance novels!*—to the man who was most likely her dream man, she wasn't quite ready to speak it into existence. Was she shy about it? Possibly, even though Toni, of all people, was sure to understand. She'd been married twice, unlike Chrissy, who hadn't even been in a single long-term relationship.

"And?"

Chrissy sighed again. Of course, Toni wanted more information. Who wouldn't?

"And after I ghosted him seven months ago, I don't feel sure about anything with him anymore. I mean, nothing's changed, has it? He's still the same man he was back then, and I'm still me. What if I mess up again? It's hard enough understanding why he's giving me a second chance, but the thought of screwing up is making me feel even more nervous than usual."

A short pause, then Toni said, "What else, Chrissy?"

Bollocks! Sorry Aunt Clare! Maybe she should have tried to figure this out on her own. Toni was just too bloody smart—if her Aunt Clare could read minds from a distance, she'd be in the hot seat for swearing and no doubt about it—for her.

"It's just a lot, Toni. I'm not the sort of woman who hangs off him at these things backstage. And I don't like it when they touch him and get up in his face like they did that one time I was there. Which is ridiculous because we're not an item and he doesn't belong to me, so I have no say in how he is or what he does with other women." She took a deep breath and confessed the rest. "And I'm not sure how well I'll handle having anyone noticing that I'm there with him if he chooses to acknowledge me in that way."

"Do you really think he'll ignore you, Chrissy? Because if you do, then you should definitely call off the plans for afterwards and just go to the concert."

Toni's tone had dropped its teasing quality. She was in counselor mode now. Chrissy had heard it often enough when she was with clients, before she took them into her office for the parts of the conversation that no one but she and the woman in question were allowed to hear.

"No. I think he'll do exactly the opposite. Which is why I'm so worried."

Toni chuckled. "You might be the only woman on the planet who's worried about being thought to be in a relationship with a rockstar, girl."

And that was no less than the truth. She was being kind of an arse, wasn't she, letting her fears get the better of her? Rory had been clear as to his intentions, and she wasn't being fair to him to question them, especially not after how well he'd treated her last night and this morning, how tender he'd been, how transparent. It was time to move forward again. Making new friends had only been the first step on the road to building her confidence as a woman. Now there was a man pursuing her, a man she wanted to have for herself. She had to do better than she was doing now, panicking on the phone with her friend about being seen with him.

"You're right. And I'm sorry for making a nuisance of myself. I'm sure you have better things to do on a Saturday morning than hold my hand while I swoon like an inexperienced Regency damsel."

Toni's laugh was infectious, and Chrissy joined her after a moment. "So you think the ripped jeans with the band tee and the leather vest are a good choice?" It didn't hurt to be sure.

"They're the perfect choice. All the band members will love that you're wearing their merch, and I'd bet good money that Rory will love the jeans."

"Okay. And I just remembered. I have a ball cap with just his face stitched on it. It's black, so it'll go well with the outfit."

"Perfect! That's one way to show him you're not running away this time."

The weight of anxiety that had been pressing in on her began to ease. "Thanks, Toni. I appreciate you wasting good husband time on me. Please tell Niall thanks as well. I know he's probably not too thrilled with you leaving him to shore up my disintegrating self-confidence."

"You're on speaker. Tell him yourself."

Chrissy made a face, glad that Toni couldn't see, but she spoke up anyway. Niall was a sweetheart of a guy, even though he was physically intimidating, and she liked him.

"Thanks for letting me steal Toni away for a bit, Niall. I hope you guys have a great weekend."

"Any time, Chrissy, and thanks. I'm sure we'll have as great a weekend as it sounds like you're going to have."

What? Did he hear...? No, she couldn't imagine Toni letting him hear what she'd told her in confidence.

"Are you guys going to the concert, as well?" That had to be what he meant, though Toni hadn't said as much.

"We are, yes. But no after-party. He's all yours, love."

His voice was teasing at the end, and she figured he could put two and two together because he was, after all, an investigator. That was his day job.

"You're so kind," she said drily, trying to project a cool vibe.

"I know," he retorted with a laugh before adding, "Here's Toni, again."

"We'll probably see each other at some point in the evening, so we can do some selfies. You know, pictures or it didn't happen?"

Chrissy laughed. "I know. But why didn't you tell me you were going, too?"

"Because I didn't find out until you did just now."

Chrissy heard Niall's voice in the background, and Toni's answering him, though what she said was muffled, and then her friend came back on.

"Anyway, I have to go. We have things to do before the show. See you later."

When her doorbell rang at precisely six that evening, Chrissy ran her hands over her thighs and draped the cute little crossbody clutch with her purse and cell phone over her shoulder. Smiling at the gorgeous man waiting to drive her to the venue—was everyone associated with the band good-looking?—she locked her door and dropped the key into the clutch.

"Thank you," she told him when he helped her out of the car half an hour later.

"You're welcome, Ms. Marcus. Enjoy the show!"

A security guard escorted her inside past the crew who were working the show. No one seemed to take note of her arrival or progress along the hallway to the dressing rooms, and when the guard handed her over to one of the band's bodyguards, whom she recognized from the last time, she let herself relax. Finally, a familiar face.

"Good evening, Ms. Marcus. How are you doing this evening?"

He was an older guy with a rich, mellow voice that somehow seemed to fit him as well as his salt-and-pepper hair.

"I'm doing okay, thank you, Mr. Pierce. How about you?" Thank God she remembered his name!

His eyes widened slightly at that, as though he was as surprised as she was that she remembered him and that she returned the courtesy he'd extended with his question. His smile made her glad she had.

"I'm doing really well, thank you." He turned and knocked on the door with a big black star on it. "Go right in. He's expecting you."

"Thanks."

She smiled at him again before stepping in through the door he held open for her and waiting until he'd closed it behind her to look around. Rory was relaxing in the loveseat, one leg draped casually over the other, watching her with a smile on his face. He took her in from head to toe, reminding her of what she'd decided to wear, and a spurt of anxiety tried to bubble up but she squashed it. She trusted Toni that she'd look good in her outfit. When she dared to look him in the eye, she saw that she'd been right to trust her friend.

"Come here, love."

Rory beckoned for her to join him, and when she reached him, he pulled her down next to him, wrapping an arm around her shoulders and pulling her in to his side.

"You look delicious, sweetheart," he told her just before he took her lips. "Delicious and all mine," he continued when he released her lips. He cast his eyes over her from the top of her head to her knees and ended with a smirk, "Love the hat and the t-shirt."

He leaned in again, turning her fully so he could kiss her properly. She let him do what he wanted to with her mouth, pulling away only when she needed air. He was breathing as hard as she was, but there was a satisfied smile on his face as he stroked her cheeks with his thumbs, cupping her face as he did so.

"You're fucking beautiful, love, and don't you ever forget it."

One last quick kiss, and then he stood up and headed over to a small table that she hadn't noticed before. There was a covered tray, a few bottles of water, and an ice bucket on it. He pulled the cover off the tray to reveal a charcuterie board full of protein-rich goodies ... hard and soft cheeses, meats, crackers, olives, and several different types of fruit.

"I waited for you before having my pre-concert snack. We tend to use up a lot of calories during a show, so it's important that we not go out there running on empty, and we only just finished up the sound checks and rehearsal."

"I thought that you'd be warming up your voice or doing meditation or something," she said, only half joking. "Don't they say every band has its pre-show rituals?"

"I've heard that, too. We don't have one, really, unless you consider keeping to ourselves to get in the right headspace for the show a ritual." He handed her a plate and said, "Please, help yourself, love."

While she took a few slices of the fruits, added some cheese and some crackers, Rory took some of everything on the board and took two bottles of water.

"Come on, let's sit and eat."

"So you guys don't do *anything* together before a show?" she wondered as she nibbled on a slice of peach.

"Just before every show, one of us will ask 'Who's on first?' and we all laugh like lunatics as we're going on stage."

Chrissy chuckled. "That sounds like a hilarious ritual, but I guess the laughing helps to relax you or something."

"Or something. It helps relieve nervous tension, which isn't the same as stage fright. And once we've done that first song, we're in the zone."

She ate a few pieces of cheese with some grapes, watching him wolf down the food on his plate.

"Why don't you have a real meal if you're so hungry?" she asked curiously.

"A real meal would be too much. We need energy, but we don't want to be sluggish, and too much food would have exactly that effect."

They finished eating, but there was still some food left on the board. She wondered if it would get thrown out but didn't want to ask. She sincerely hoped that that was not the case.

"Show starts in an hour, love." A knock sounded. "Come."

The man who walked in was Chrissy's height, but he was pencil thin and seemed to glow all over.

"Ah, Christina Marcus, meet Paul Wilson. Paul, Chrissy."

Rory headed to the small table next to the loveseat, and while he settled himself on the stool, Paul adjusted the light, and Chrissy realized that he was there to do Rory's makeup.

"How are you, Ms. Marcus? Excited for the show?"

"I'm fine, thank you, Mr. Wilson. And yes, I'm very excited to be here."

His smile was sharp, almost searching, as if he were on the hunt for something he would only find in her face. Chrissy held his gaze for a moment before turning away. When he was focused on Rory, she looked back to where they were, watching him work his magic to transform

Rory into the edgy, sexy rockstar whom the women screamed for, whether he was singing a head-banging song or a soulful, romantic ballad.

Half an hour later, when he was done, Chrissy secretly admitted to being jealous of her lover. His already gorgeous features had taken on a quiet drama that would make them stand out under the harsh, bright lights onstage.

"That's really beautiful," she blurted out when Paul began to pack away his supplies.

He looked up, a different, warmer smile on his face. "Thank you. Your man's smooth, even features make it easy."

Chrissy's eyes widened at his description, and he smirked but said nothing else in response.

"See you around, Ro. Nice to meet you, Ms. Marcus. Enjoy the show!"

He stepped out, closing the door quietly behind him as Rory stepped over to her.

"You okay?"

His eyes were shadowed with concern. He was probably wondering how she was feeling about what Paul had said.

"I'm fine. And if you're asking if I'm okay with what Paul said, then yes, I am."

"Good."

He added nothing else, only pulling a sleeveless black leather vest over the plain white tee he was wearing above ripped black jeans and black boots. His fingers flashed with what she assumed were either silver or platinum rings, and he wore a black fedora from under which his golden hair spilled in a kind of messy halo around his face. Chrissy was mesmerized by his absolute beauty.

"Ready, love?"

She blinked and nodded, going ahead of him out the door where the other band members were waiting. Except for Tristan, each man had a woman with him, and Chrissy supposed these women were their wives or girlfriends. Her chest warmed at the thought that she was now one of them, even though Rory hadn't asked and she hadn't agreed to any name for what they were building. Apparently, Paul was right ... she *was* his woman.

Toni and Niall were already in the roped area backstage where she and the other guests would watch the show. She hugged the couple, and shook hands with the wives and John's fiancée, settling to watch the opening act warm up the crowd for the guys. Then it was their turn. Rory turned to her, his eyes holding a question as he looked at her lips. She nodded. After all they'd done together over the last twenty-four hours, a kiss couldn't hurt, and she didn't think the people there who knew her would care.

He bussed her lips and whispered, "Thanks, love."

"Break a leg, Rory," she whispered back, smiling at him.

The concert was a roaring success, from Rory's shouted "Hello, London!" to his final "We love you, London. Goodnight!" Every song pulled her further under the spell of the music, under the spell of the man who sang of love and heartbreak, of passion, desire, and hope. She sang along when they played some of her favorites and listened enraptured when they debuted their newest single.

"Darling, give me just another moment,
Before the whole world closes in,
Let me lay my love upon you, baby,
Lay all my heart and soul out on the line.

Never want to know another moment
Without you at the center of my soul
Never want to spend another sunrise
Where you're not beside me in my arms."

Tears welled in Chrissy's eyes. The song spoke of a tender longing for something the singer thought was probably not in the cards. It was a wish, a prayer, a supplication. Ballads always pulled some of the deepest emotions from her, and this one was no exception. Surreptitiously wiping the escaping tears away, she listened as Rory moved into the first refrain.

"Spaces in between, that is where our love shines,
Spaces in between, baby will you stay mine?"

His voice deepened, if that were possible, as if he were romancing the woman he loved in the song. Her body warmed at that thought. She didn't know if he loved her, but he had certainly loved on her the night before, and the idea that he might be singing to her was an unexpected turn-on. She hoped no one was watching her, because she was a mess of tears and smiles, which wasn't what she imagined a sophisticated woman would be showing to the world at that moment.

Someone handed her a little packet of tissues. She looked up, forgetting how she might appear, to find Toni smiling at her.

"Thank you."

She cleaned up, wiping instead of blowing her nose because, with her luck, she'd be blowing her trumpet at the quietest part of the song and the whole world would hear. Not to mention it would ruin the performance. She couldn't take that chance. She managed to keep it together for the rest of the show, though her heart rate never decreased, and her body ached for his touch as she watched him play and sing and move across the stage.

The crowd roared after their last song, and two encores in, they were still chanting his name. Rory grinned widely at them, then spoke over the noise, "We are Third Generation!" He turned and gestured to his bandmates, who began the ending spiel.

"I'm John."

"I'm William."

"I'm Henry."

"I'm Tristan."

"I'm Riordan. We love you, London! Goodnight!"

CHAPTER 15

Rory's final words carried over the crowd, who didn't stop applauding for another few minutes until the guys left the stage and the lights dimmed. Rory headed straight to where she now stood, his whole body drenched in sweat. She let her eyes roam over his wet face, his golden locks plastered to his skin, the soaked t-shirt leaving nothing to the imagination.

"You all were brilliant, Rory," she said as he stopped in front of her. "Just brilliant!"

He smiled at her but didn't answer for a moment, only leaned in and kissed her on each cheek. "Come with me."

She turned to see where Toni and Niall were. "Can I just say goodbye to them?"

"Yes. I'll come with you."

They walked over to where the couple was talking to the other members of the group. Rory reached out to shake hands.

"I'm so happy you both could make it."

"We wouldn't have missed it for the world," Niall said. "You boys are brilliant!"

"That's what I said," Chrissy chimed in with a wide smile. Looking over at the others, she gave them a thumbs up before turning back to her friends. "I just wanted to say goodnight before you left."

"I'll see you on Monday."

Toni's eyes telegraphed a message that Chrissy understood immediately: *I'll need all the gossip.* She chuckled and nodded.

"Yes, ma'am."

Niall looked between them, then looked over at Rory and said, "Is it just me, or are these two speaking in code?"

"I wouldn't be at all surprised if they were," Rory replied, laughing softly. Then he looked down at Chrissy. "Ready?"

"Yes."

She waggled her fingers at her friends and followed him to a room where the other women were already sitting and chatting amiably together. Rory stepped in for just a moment.

"Evening, ladies! This is my friend Christina. Chrissy, meet Gen, Sara, and Dawn. The lads and I will be with you all soon. Help yourselves to the food."

Chrissy looked to where he pointed and saw the table loaded with covered trays that she had missed before.

"You killed it tonight, Rory," the redhead said. "I guess I can see why, now." She cast a teasing glance in Chrissy's direction, and Rory chuckled.

"Mind your business, Dawn," he answered without heat.

Then he left and Chrissy felt the eyes of all the women on her. Dawn spoke first ... was she the spokesperson for the group?

"Hi, I'm Dawn, Will's wife. This is Gen," she pointed to a tall Asian woman, "Henry's wife, and Sara," dark-haired and gorgeous, Chrissy noted, "is John's fiancée." She paused for a second before adding, "And you are...?"

Chrissy understood at once what she was asking. How was she supposed to respond to a question she didn't have an answer for?

"Rory's friend." That was the best she could do.

The three women exchanged knowing looks before Dawn said, "We'll just take that to mean you're his girlfriend but in denial about it." She smirked and wagged a finger at Chrissy. "Just because he hasn't used the word as yet doesn't make it any less real."

Clearly not expecting a response, she turned away and walked over to the table, pulling the covers off the food. The others joined her, so Chrissy made her way over as well. There were various kinds of sandwiches, two more charcuterie boards, and fruits in a bowl. One container sat atop a heater, and when Dawn lifted the lid, there were chicken wings being kept warm.

"Help yourself, Christina."

Sara's voice was low and soft but laced with kindness. She sidled up next to Chrissy and added, so only she could hear, "Don't mind Dawn. She's harmless, just unapologetically nosy."

Chrissy smiled, feeling less anxious at this show of acceptance. "I'll remember that, thanks."

While they ate, they talked about the show, and Chrissy was grateful that she wasn't in the spotlight anymore. Gen was the quietest of the lot, rarely speaking but gifting them with sweet smiles when Dawn's commentary was especially amusing. It wasn't as awkward as she had feared it would be when Rory had left her with them, and by the time the men walked in, freshly showered and changed, she was relaxed and laughing at something Dawn had just said.

"You boys must be starving," Dawn said.

"We are," her husband replied, going over to leave a smacking kiss on her lips. "What's good?"

"Everything, love," she told him, giving him a wink that made Chrissy smile.

Her answer earned her another, deeper kiss, and the love they had for each other seemed to pour out of them and bathe the room in warmth.

"You know what they say," Tris said with a smirk, helping himself to food. "Get a room."

General laughter followed his teasing comment, and once the men had their food, they settled down next to their women. Tristan sat with Henry and Gen, and Chrissy watched the three of them, noting how the couple treated him with affection. She remembered that he was the most reserved of the group, and she could see why he would gravitate toward Gen, who was like him in so many ways.

"You alright, love?" Rory called her attention back to him.

"I'm fine. How do you feel?"

"Like I've been through the wringer, to be honest."

His eyes were tired and his face a little paler than usual, but his smile was as warm as ever, and the look on his face as he watched her take stock of him was open and affectionate. He had changed into another white t-shirt and faded blue jeans, but no leather vest and only a thick silver choker and a couple of rings. He still looked amazing, like the rockstar he was.

"What do you have coming up?"

"We'll take a day or two to rest, but then it's back to work on the studio album and rehearsals for the North American tour starting next January."

"I hope you'll rest, Rory," she said earnestly. "You worked really hard up there tonight."

"And we've got to go out and see the fans for a bit before we can go home." He put down the sandwich he was eating and looked at her. "Are you okay to stay with me, or do you want James to take you home?"

"I thought I was spending the night..."

Her words trailed off. She didn't want anyone to overhear what she was saying to him, especially if she had misunderstood. Had he only meant for her to spend the one night? Or had he had his fill and needed her gone? She would leave without a fuss, if that was what he wanted, but it would be the last time she saw him. She wasn't going to let anyone, not even the man she suspected had stolen her heart, take her for granted or play her for a fool.

"You are, love," he reassured her, apparently noticing the change in her mood. "But I also don't want you to wait around watching fans get stupid with me. I know it upsets you."

It definitely did, without question, but if the other band members' partners managed to keep their love alive and glowing despite the challenges that fame brought with it—she remembered Dawn and Will—why couldn't she learn how to do the same?

"I'd rather stay with you." That was the truth, even if the thought of being in the spotlight made her nerves quake.

"Alright. You'll stay in here with the ladies. No one will see you until we're ready to leave, okay? And you know what to do then. Answer no questions, just smile and walk with me out to the limo."

Chrissy nodded. She could do this. Afterwards, she'd try not to overthink it, and hopefully, she'd feel better about it in the morning. Finished with the light meal, Rory and his mates left to greet their fans, sign autographs, and take pictures. She knew it could take up to an hour, and given the rousing reception they'd had during the show, she wouldn't be surprised if there were a lot of fans waiting patiently to meet their idols.

Dawn went to switch on the television so they could watch the goings-on without having to be there themselves. The reception room was crowded, so much so that the men had to wait until security made a path for them to make their way to the front. Then people could visit with their favorites. She kept her eyes on Rory, who smiled and laughed, signed autographs, and posed for pictures with everyone it looked like.

Once or twice, she thought she saw women trying to kiss him—because standing next to him for the photo op wasn't enough, apparently—but his bodyguard stopped those attempts, and the women lost their chance for a selfie with him. She wasn't mad about that at all. Even if she was not prepared to speak the words aloud, Rory was hers, and she didn't share. How dare they think they could put their hands and lips on him?

Eventually, the men left the still-lingering guests, returning to get their women. Chrissy assumed that there would be fans milling around outside, waiting for one last glimpse of them, and she steeled herself to walk the gauntlet—as she thought of it—even though it was not far from the entrance to the limousines waiting to take them away. She ignored the fans' wolf whistles, applause, and shouted comments and questions, especially those directed at Rory, who didn't respond, just waved and smiled until they were safely shut into the car they were sharing with Tristan, Will, and Dawn.

"Alright?" he asked, pulling her into his side.

"Yes, thanks." It hadn't been as bad as she'd feared. Maybe she had matured in the last seven months.

"Good."

It was clear that the men were tired, though they laughed and joked the whole way, as each band member was dropped off at his own home. Rory's was the last stop, and once they were indoors, he led her upstairs immediately, chucking his duffel into a corner before turning to pull her into his arms. The kiss was hungry. Chrissy felt the same need and opened to him, letting him take what he wanted.

"Do you need anything? I'm going to get an after-midnight snack."

"I can come with..."

"No, love. I need you to be waiting for me when I get back. In that." She looked behind her to where he was pointing and saw a t-shirt laid out on the bed. "You looked good in my shirt last night. I'm aiming for a repeat."

"Okay." She wasn't going to argue, even if she could. But as her heart was racing again and her limbs were beginning to shake a little, it was a good thing he didn't seem to expect more of an answer.

As soon as he walked out, she raced into his bathroom, suddenly overcome. Relieving herself, she washed her hands and wondered if she should clean up a bit. After all, he'd had a shower before coming home and she hadn't. She didn't want any offensive body odors to turn him off, because she liked a turned-on Rory a whole lot.

Decision made, she set the water temperature, went to get the t-shirt she'd be sleeping in, stripped, and stepped into the shower. She'd be smelling like Rory when she got into bed, but she didn't care. He always smelled delicious, anyway, so that was a win. She had meant to take a quick shower, but the water felt so good that she closed her eyes and let it wash over her, careful to keep her hair away. She didn't have the things she'd need to deal with her hair if it got wet.

When hard hands reached around her to squeeze her breasts before moving lower to cup her feminine mound, she gasped in shock.

"Rory!" she shrieked.

"You're bloody gorgeous, d'you know that?"

He slid a finger between the lips of her sex, pressing in and circling the bundle of nerves that had her hitching up onto her tiptoes and opening her legs in invitation. When had she become such a wanton? She didn't know, but she suspected it had a lot to do with the man fondling her and sending a finger up inside her.

"Rory..." What was she going to say again? She couldn't think with him driving her slowly up to another peak of pleasure.

"I want you to come for me before we go to bed, love. Then I'm going to suck and lick you, fuck you and make love to you, and send you flying over and over before we sleep."

Dirty, dirty words, filthy promises ... she was all for that. They made her heartbeat increase and her temperature rise. They stroked her and sent her body into overdrive, loosening her legs even more and making her want to do the same to the man currently stopping her from collapsing to the shower floor.

"Oh goodness!" she exclaimed when Rory slid three fingers into her, nailing her g-spot when he did and sliding his thumb over her clitoris at the same time.

The double assault pushed her up and over the edge and she screamed into his mouth as she came and came, unable even to return his kisses. He kept finger fucking her, though he slacked off her clit when she hissed at that touch. It was too much, but she never wanted him to stop invading her wet flesh with his hard digits. All that was left was for him to plunge into her with the erection she felt pressing against her.

"Rory, please!"

"Please what, little kitten? Tell me what you want. I'll give you anything you ask for."

He pulled out of her, planting a searing kiss on her lips before kneeling at her feet and kissing *those* lips as well. His tongue laved her folds, sliding soothingly over her little button, seeking entry into her depths and sending her pulse racing again before it had even settled down. He fed from her until she was ready to fall over the edge again, but this time, he left her there, teetering on the brink.

"Come."

His voice was rough with lust. She let him do whatever he wanted, since she was a little lost in her own head. He turned the water off and stepped out of the shower, pulling her after him. She was still in a daze, so he dried her off and patted her bottom.

"Put that on and go wait for me in bed. I'll be right there."

She pulled on the t-shirt, this one with a smiling Rory and his band name on the front and settled herself against the headboard. She saw the snack he'd brought up to share ... grapes and a hard cheese, and wine. She knew if she had any of the wine, she'd be snoring in no time, and she wasn't planning on any of that until after...

Rory walked out of the bathroom as she was processing that thought and it stalled in her head. He was wearing a black silk robe which he'd left open so she could see he was wearing nothing under it, hence her momentary inability to think. Her pulse kicked up again. Could a person have a heart attack if her heart kept racing like that? She really hoped not. She wanted to be present and aware for everything that Rory planned to do to her tonight.

"Scoot over, love," he said, getting into the big bed beside her and pulling the tray across his lap. "Help yourself."

While she put some grapes and a couple of pieces of cheese onto a napkin, he poured the wine and put the bottle back on his bedside table. Handing her a glass, he said, "To making memories."

She looked at him curiously. "I don't mind toasting to that, but why?"

He leaned in and kissed her cheek. "Because I never want to forget anything we've done together this weekend. And I want you always to remember them, as well." His eyes were full of warm affection.

"To making memories," she repeated, and sipped the wine.

Rory fed her the grapes and cheese, and when she shook her head when he tried to offer her the wine, he asked, "Why not, sweetheart?"

"I'm especially lightheaded with wine, and if I drink this whole glass, I'll be asleep before you can say 'fuck.'"

Her eyes widened as soon as the word left her lips. Who was this loose-lipped woman and what had she done with Chrissy? Rory's laughter did not ease her embarrassment in the slightest, and even after he apologized—"I'm not laughing at you, love," though he absolutely was, the bastard!—she still felt mortified by what she'd let escape her lips.

When he finally got his amusement under control, he said, "What if I promise to make it so you won't feel the effects of the wine, hmm? If I make it so all you'll feel is me? If I make it so *I'm* the one who makes you fall asleep?"

He could definitely make good on that last promise, as she knew from very recent experience.

"The wine will relax you, but I will wear you out in the best way possible, little kitten. What do you say? Trust me?"

Seduction was the melody under the lyrics he spoke in her ear, and she gave in without even trying to resist. There really was no point, right? She wanted everything he was prepared to give her. She was greedy for it. She would not, *could* not say no.

"Yes."

He stole another quick and dirty kiss, then held her glass to her lips. She sipped a bit more this time, and she finished her snack like that. He hadn't eaten anything as yet, and she deemed it appropriate to reciprocate the tender attention he had just paid to her.

"What about *your* snack?" she asked. "I'd like to return the favor."

He grinned as though she'd just given him a much-anticipated gift. "I'll let you do whatever you want as soon as you come sit on me." He moved the tray off his lap to the side table.

Memories of the first time she'd ridden him, his cock sliding against her intimately, had her moving at once to straddle his lap, coloring up at the thought of their naked bodies touching in that most private of places. She had fit him like a hand in a glove, her warm, heavy lips wrapping around his steely cock in a welcoming, erotic embrace. She moaned now as she felt his hardness snug up against her folds, and she forgot why she was there for a moment, settling herself atop him and sliding her sex against his length with a slow roll of her hips.

Rory hissed and pushed up, leaning in to capture her lips. They kissed deeply for a moment before Chrissy remembered why she'd climbed aboard. She pulled away, inhaling sharply and reaching for the plate of grapes and cheese. It would be difficult to concentrate on feeding him when she really only wanted to slide up and down his pole like a striptease dancer at a sex club, but she would give it her best shot.

After all, what did she have to lose if she missed a few grapes and some cheese? The better question was, what did she have to gain? The cock nestled between her lips swelled, as though Rory knew what she was thinking, and she moaned. Time to hurry up the feeding.

CHAPTER 16

*S*he's gonna kill me. Rory groaned as Chrissy rolled her hips again. He was on a knife edge of desire, needing to pierce her to the core of her being, to rut against her, to fuck her into nirvana. But she was trying to be romantic, as he had been, and feed him before they got down and dirty. He should really let her do her thing, right?

He sucked in the grape she held to his lips as well as the two fingers she held it between. She groaned with him as he suckled her, giving them both one last hard suck before releasing them. She slid over him again and he gripped her hips, keeping her there but stilling her movements.

"If you want me to finish these, you'll have to stop teasing me, kitten," he told her, doing his best to keep his tone even.

There wasn't much he could do about the rapid beating of his heart or the slight panting that he had going on, though, and if she was a quick study, she'd know exactly why his cool demeanor was a bold-faced lie. He held her gaze and watched as she cocked her head to the side, as if she were contemplating a weighty idea.

Then she bit the side of her bottom lip and asked, "Do you *want* to finish them?"

Hell, no. I want to finish you! Patience ... that's what he needed in this moment. "I want whatever will make you happy, love." There, that sounded reasonable, right? "So if you want to feed me, I'm all for it."

She smiled, a sweet but secret smile that he couldn't read, because it dazzled him, and he lost a little more of his heart to her in that moment. She leaned in and he held himself perfectly still, expecting a kiss and shocked when she bypassed his waiting lips to whisper in his ear, "What if I want to feed you something else?"

Her breath was hot in his ear, on the lobes, down the side of his face. And her body was on the move again. He stifled another groan and waited, sensing that there was more where that had come from. She may have begun as an inexperienced woman, but she was finally letting her instinctual passion rule and bring out the foxy, feisty lover he suspected she had hidden all her life.

"Or what if ..." She paused to lick his earlobe, and this time he couldn't stop the groan that escaped. "What if I want you to feed *me* something else, as well?"

The words came out in a rush, as if she was speaking on the fly without thinking about what came out of her mouth. It seemed like she was losing control, and the things she was saying and doing were not something she might otherwise have done. But if she was serious, and wanted to learn how to please him with her lips and tongue, who was he to argue? He didn't have the strength to refuse, so he'd just have to teach her. *Poor me ... such a hardship!*

He pulled back to look her in the eye, seeing the stark hunger there. She had picked up the pace, her hips rolling in a steady rhythm over his cock now, and the sight of her pleasuring herself, using his body to bring her ecstasy, set him ablaze. He rolled with her, letting the head of his dick bump up against her clitoris, and rubbing her there, going faster, taking over the dance, and she clearly forgot all about feeding him anything except her tongue and her breath.

Rory took the plate from her boneless fingers and placed it back on the bedside table. He was done eating anything that wasn't on Chrissy's body.

"You like this, don't you, sweetheart?" he murmured as he rode her clit with his cock-head. "Like it when I rub you like this. Does it make you hornier? Make you wanna cum for me? Slather me with all those sweet juices from your pussy? Hmm?"

She gasped as though his words were some kind of fuel, igniting her nerve endings and swelling the fountain of pleasure waiting to burst inside her. The way she sped up with him, moaning and sighing and gasping for air, meant he wasn't even going to bother teaching her how to give a blowjob until after he'd brought them both over the edge. Which meant he needed to be inside her. Now.

Remembering about protection at the last second, he reached over and snagged a condom from his nightstand drawer, slid it on hurriedly, his hands shaking with the urgency he was feeling, and then held her body above his so he could slide into her. She settled her bottom against his thighs, mewling in pleasure when he jerked his cock inside her without moving in any other way.

"Rory, please move. I need you to move."

Which, given that he needed the same thing, was better than good. He moved, holding her thighs down while he thrust up into her, ramming her hard, over and over, growling as the desire built inside him and the pleasure peaked. He fucked her hard and deep, speeding up his thrusts when she let herself go completely and rode his dick like a champion. Every upward stroke drew a sigh from her parted lips, and every downward plunge dragged out a grunt.

"Geee..." She began a long wail as her body caved. "Mayyyr ... Jo .... oh gawwwwd!"

Her orgasm struck her hard, robbing her of speech. The nonsense words she uttered spiked his own release, because he felt the same measure of lust, the same depth of desire, the same overwhelming fulfillment as she did as he shot into the condom. He wanted to mark her with his seed, to own her, so she would know for always that she was his woman, that he didn't want anyone else, that she was more than enough for him, the best thing to ever happen to him.

He rolled with her, slamming her onto the bed beneath him, and kept plunging into her, changing the angle of his thrusts until he was pegging her g-spot with every stroke. He bared his teeth at the ecstasy that shot through his entire body when he broke, crying out her name as he came. Cum filled the condom, so much that Rory feared it would leak over the sides. He couldn't stop cumming, couldn't stop fucking her, couldn't stop, period. *Oh fuck!*

Finally, finally, his balls emptied themselves and he lay still, too weak to move but trying not to rest his full weight on her. He had wrecked her, he knew, but he was in no better shape. His breathing was as labored as hers was, his heart pounding in his chest, his arms and legs trembling in solidarity. This thing between them was about more than sex, he knew, but god, it was also about the most mind-blowing sex.

Chrissy's grip on him tightened when he tried to roll off her, so he let her hold him to her body, feeling the sweat cooling between them, feeling her heart rate slow, feeling her limbs soften. She had dozed off, and he kissed her cheek tenderly before rolling to the side, keeping his arm over her and watching her sleep. He'd wake her in a few, but these few minutes, when he could be alone with her in this completely unguarded state, were pure and innocent, a world away from the unfettered fury and power of her lust and passion.

He wasn't foolish enough to imagine that a few hard shags would change her from the reserved, self-conscious person she had been all her life, but he was confident that he'd put a big dent in them, that she was ready to be more than she'd ever allowed herself to be before. And he would be there for it all, if she'd let him. She stirred, and when her eyes fluttered open and found his gaze, she smiled.

Rory's heart stuttered at the shy, sweet beauty of it as it transformed her face from very pretty to absolutely ravishing.

"Hey. Ready to clean up?"

He leaned in to hear her whispered, "Yeah," and her warm breath was an erotic touch on his cheek. He ached to kiss into that breath, to mingle it with his own, but he resisted. Instead, he rolled away from her to dispose of the condom and wet a washcloth to clean her up. Her eyes had closed again when he got back to the bed.

"Come on then, love."

He cleaned between her thighs before rolling her back onto her side. He would let her rest before taking her again. Disposing of the washcloth, he slid in next to her and pulled her back against his chest. She sighed in evident contentment, making Rory smile as he let himself slide into sleep with her.

He was still tired when the clanging of his cellphone ringing woke him to bright sunlight a couple of hours after a third session of wild lovemaking. He scrambled to answer it, almost falling out of bed, and prayed he hadn't woken Chrissy. He stood up and walked over to the window seat and settled his spine against the wall.

"Yeah!"

He answered without looking to see who was calling, his voice rusty with irritation and exhaustion. Who the fuck would choose to call him the day after his last concert when everyone who had his number knew he always slept in then?

"Sorry to wake you, mate, but I thought you should get a heads-up. Check your messages. I've sent you some links you need to see. I'm sorry, mate. I know how this is likely to go down when your lady sees them. Call me if you need me."

His manager hung up before Rory could ask what he was going on about, so he did what the man suggested and checked his messages. There were three links ... one to Twitter, one to Instagram, and one to TikTok. The images must have been taken by one or more random peepers instead of the paparazzi, but how did anyone not cleared to be backstage have gotten any of these photos? Clearly, the crew could not all be trusted.

He clicked on the TikTok link, curious more than anxious to see what was there. "Back in the limelight again!" That was the first caption, under the video clip of him kissing Chrissy after the show, with an audio clip of the title to Kina's "Can We Kiss Forever?" The angle at which the shot was taken made it appear as though he'd been kissing her on the lips. Choosing not to read the comments, he moved on to the second set of images, taken before and after the show and posted on Twitter.

He was smiling down into her eyes in the first one, kissing her gently on the lips—there could be no mistaking that one—waving at her as he went up on stage with the lads. In the second one, he was waving goodbye to the audience before leaving the stage at the end of the show. The caption for them read, "Riordan slays after claiming his mystery lady!"

He huffed. Why did people care so much about who he was seeing? It was bad enough his mother thought she should concern herself with his love life, but strangers doing it was an imposition. He understood why Chrissy hated the limelight, he really did, and even though he had come to terms with it as part of his job, he still didn't like it.

The third set, on Instagram, was a series of four shots, the first the same as the one taken by the paparazzi seven months earlier. He had his arm around Chrissy, holding her close to his side, and looking down into her face as they waited for the others outside the venue. That had freaked her out because the captions back then had ranged from the silly to the salacious. He refused to rehash them now. Best to see what the damage was this time.

That first shot in the set was the professional one. It was followed by the two taken the night before, the kiss to her lips before, and the two to her cheeks afterwards. The last was a shot of them getting into the limousine, his hand at her back. The caption for the lot said, "Has Riordan finally fallen for champion of battered women?" His eyes widened. He went back, looking more closely at each photo, wondering how they knew where Chrissy worked. And that's when he saw the person who may have inadvertently given away her secret.

In the second picture, taken just before he went on stage, he could make out Toni and Niall just to Chrissy's right. Niall had gained a bit of notoriety after Toni's ex had almost killed him in a hit-and-run. And as the trial began and Niall and his partner were brought in as Crown witnesses against the man, the media had, of course, sought every opportunity to sensationalize the case even more than it already was by digging into Niall's life enough to know that his now-wife worked at Hope House.

Rory could think of no other reason for Chrissy's job to have been discovered. "Must be a slow news week," he muttered to himself, deciding to read some of the comments for this one. His alarm increased when he saw that at least one of her coworkers was not shy about sharing in her unintended moments of fame by mentioning Hope House in her comments on the pictures. At least she hadn't offered up her name as well, though anyone who wanted to know could find out much more easily now.

He sighed heavily, shutting down his phone and looking back to where Chrissy was now stirring in bed. She'd wake soon, and he'd have to let her know, but he had no idea how she would respond. It wasn't as though the captions were especially intrusive, but that they existed at all would feel like an invasion of privacy to her, he felt sure. And he was also sure that that had been a part of why she'd turned tail before and left him eating her dust.

They needed to talk. He loved that she'd given her body completely to him, that she'd trusted him with something that was clearly important to her. But he wanted it all ... her body, her mind, her heart. He wanted to test the theory that everyone has a soulmate, because he wanted her to be the one for him.

Unerringly, his mind went back fifteen years, to the young man working with a small theater company in their pit orchestra who fell for the lead actress in the last musical he worked in before he started the band. Two years post-graduation with a First Class Bachelors and a Masters in Music Composition and Performance, he had been still unsure of what direction to take, and the ensuing fight with his father—which was still ongoing— had made his job his only refuge. And then he'd met her.

Melanie Bynum had not been his first lover, but she had been his first true love. He fell for her after her first rehearsal, when it was clear that she was not only a consummate professional, but that she had a heart of gold to match her talent. And she had been the one to show him how to live his life the way he wanted to instead of trying to please his parents. She herself had been estranged from her parents since her uni days, and he was in awe of her. A year younger than his twenty-three years, she had a depth and a maturity to her that he envied.

He should have known she was too good for him, or perhaps that he was not enough for her. Would things be different if they'd met now? Perhaps ... he was a success at what he'd chosen to do with his life, and she had advanced in her career and was now a much-sought-after star of stage and screen. He should probably have waited longer than three months to ask her to move in with him, and certainly longer than six months to ask her to marry him. He'd been much too young and naive to have made a marriage work then.

Now, though, he was different. He knew it like he knew his times tables, like he knew the notes that went with the lyrics of every song he'd ever written, like he knew he had a gift of music that it was his privilege to share with the world. He knew he could make a marriage work today. And if pressed, he would admit that he wanted to make a marriage with Chrissy work more than he wanted anything else in the world.

"Are you alright?"

The subject of his thoughts stood next to him, his t-shirt hanging off one shoulder, the hem reaching her knees. She looked sleep-rumpled and sexy as hell, her dusky skin glowing in the morning light. He smiled at her, not really knowing how to answer her loaded question. So many thoughts were vying for space in his tired brain, and he didn't want to say the wrong thing, and lying to her would be absolutely the wrong thing.

"I don't know," he said honestly. "It depends on how you're going to react to the news."

Her brows furrowed in confusion. She was still not completely awake, as the yawn that escaped her made clear. Rory wished he didn't have to tell her anything other than how much he wanted a repeat of their night's play, but he knew it would be irresponsible of him not to do so. When all was said and done, the social media stories were nothing but a nuisance to him, but they would be so much more to Chrissy. And he knew that Chrissy's comfort would always be his first concern. And here he was back at honesty again.

"There's something I need you to see, sweetheart. Come, sit with me."

He slid one leg up onto the seat and guided her down in front of him, keeping the other on the ground. Then he pulled her back against him, urging her to put both her legs up so she'd be comfortable. Once they were settled against each other, Rory opened his phone and showed her the links. He didn't let go of her, wrapping his arm around her, dropping light kisses in her hair, stroking the soft skin above her elbow, doing his best to be a soothing presence behind her as she took in the articles.

"I thought there were no reporters backstage before the show," was her first comment.

Okay, so she wasn't panicking. That was a good sign, right?

"There weren't supposed to be, and to be fair, these look more like pictures people took on their phones than anything else, except for the one from seven months ago." He sighed again. "Which doesn't make it any better. Those guys know they're not supposed to do that without permission."

"What if they were paid to do it?" she wanted to know next.

Another great question. "It's possible, I suppose."

He studied her face, looking for signs that she was distressed. He couldn't see anything like that, but then, she had schooled her features so nothing at all was showing, and before he could try to probe her for other reactions, she stood up and walked away to the bathroom, closing the door quietly behind her. Was she panicking in there now, away from his eyes? Could he barge in to check on her? Maybe he should give her a few minutes on her own before resorting to such drastic measures.

While he was debating how much time was enough before he staged an intervention, his phone rang again. This time he checked it before he answered. It was Toni.

"Hi, Rory, it's Toni. I'm sorry to be calling you on your day off, but I'm worried about Chrissy. Have you seen the pictures online?"

"Yeah, I have, and so has she. I just showed them to her."

"Where is she? Can I talk to her?"

"She's in the bathroom. I'll have her call you when she gets out."

He had no intention of telling her that Chrissy had been in the bathroom for a good ten minutes already, and that he was getting ready to go get her himself. He knew that Toni probably had a better chance than he did of talking her off any emotional ledge she was currently hanging from, but she was his, dammit, and *he* wanted to be the one to calm her down. Assuming she was upset, and so far, the evidence hadn't suggested that she was. He paused to listen closely. If she were bawling her eyes out, he would hear her, wouldn't he? He got up and went over to the door, getting to it just as she opened it and looked up at him. Restraining the urge to reach for her, he used his words instead.

"Are you alright, love?"

"I'm fine."

She didn't look him in the eyes as she spoke. That and her clipped response were not encouraging, but she was dry-eyed, at least. He persevered. He didn't want her ghosting him again. They were too far gone down the road this time for it to be anything less than gut-wrenching for him if she did.

"I'm hoping that if you're not alright, you'll tell me, Chrissy, so we can talk about it."

She sighed, still avoiding his gaze. "What's there to talk about? Nothing they've said is terrible, is it?" When he gave in and pulled her chin up, forcing her to see him, she relented and looked him in the eye before adding, "I ... I just need time to process it. I knew it would happen again."

Relief didn't precisely describe the feeling washing over him as he let her walk past him back to the window seat. He followed her, sitting next to her, needing to feel her warmth.

"Tell me what you're thinking. Let's figure this out together."

Pickles rumbled against her side while Lynx snored lightly in her lap as Chrissy watched the video clip a third time. It had been a week since her sleepover weekend with Rory, a week since the media had begun to invade her privacy again, a week since she'd last seen Rory. At least this time, she hadn't cut him off completely. She had called him after their heart-to-heart on Sunday morning to let him know that she had enjoyed her weekend. She still remembered the sweet moments when all they did was smile at each other on the video call.

"I'm glad you enjoyed yourself, sweetheart. I did too. A lot."

Those words reverberated in her mind now as she saw what no one but the people backstage should have seen ... Rory kissing her lightly on the lips before going up on stage to begin the show. Was this what her life would be like going forward, if she chose to keep exploring this relationship with Rory? How much more intrusive would they be before they left the two of them alone?

And whom could she trust? She knew that Moira hadn't meant to out her in the comment on the images, but she had. Was it fair to expect her coworkers to have to watch their every word where she was concerned because she was dating a rockstar? She was a nobody, not a princess or anything like that.

"Sadly, it comes with the territory, love. It's a reality of my life, like going on tour, but I've learned to manage it as best I can," Rory had told her when he'd asked her to tell him what she was thinking. He'd gestured around him and out to the yard. "This house is, in a lot of ways, a beautiful prison, but it keeps the media out of my personal space as much as it can. I dislike their invasion of my privacy as much as you do, but I've learned to let it go when I can't avoid it."

Let it go ... she'd never had to ignore her feelings about anything before because there'd never been a reason to. Until now. She wasn't the same person she'd been seven months or even a month ago. A lot had changed since she and Rory had met again at Toni's wedding. And she didn't just mean her current non-virginal state, though the memory of those hours in Rory's arms, under his hands and mouth and body, still made her grow warm and needy. She felt different in her spirit as much as in her body.

And she was finally ready to admit that she had fallen for Rory months ago and had run away and used the excuse of unwanted media attention because she hadn't known what her feelings meant or how to handle their unexpected impact. She hadn't thought then that Rory's interest in her would last, especially if she didn't sleep with him. But this time, he had proven her wrong, and she needed to stop trying to put a label on *his* feelings in order to avoid facing her own.

Her phone vibrated and she picked it up, seeing it was Rory calling. He was probably almost there, and she should really dislodge her pets and change into something a little less fur-covered.

"This is Chrissy."

"Chrissy, I'll be there in five minutes. I'm bringing dinner, okay?"

"Okay."

Sighing, not sure what she was feeling but determined to snap out of her funk, she went to change into something less ratty than the thin sweatpants and t-shirt. By the time Rory knocked on her door, she was in a pair of leggings that did nothing to disguise the high curve of her bottom and a flowy top that she hoped was long enough to tame the view. She also put on a bra ... there was no promise of sexy times, and she didn't want to appear to be asking for anything other than conversation, even if her body was already heating up with thoughts of what she'd like Rory to do to her.

Rory looked like sex on a stick when she opened the door to him. She stepped away so he could pass her, noting that he hadn't driven himself this time. Trying to distract herself from the beauty of his legs encased in tight ripped jeans and his shoulders stretching a too-tight white t-shirt, she trailed him into her kitchen and asked, "Did you take a cab here?"

He put the bags he was carrying down on the counter and walked over to where she stood, pulling her into his arms before he answered her.

"I'm hoping someone will invite me for a sleepover," he told her, as if that answered her question.

Then what he said registered, and she looked up at him. "What?"

"I'd like to spend the night with you, Chrissy. So after dinner, after we talk, I'd love to stay. If," he stretched out the word, "that's okay with you?"

She looked him in the eye, ready to take the next step. Why she had thought having sex was the be-all and end-all of everything, she had no idea. This whole communicating thing, baring her heart and soul to another person ... *that* was the real deal. Not that making love with Rory hadn't been a revelation and a total joy, one that she wanted to repeat over and over, but she knew that that secret wish would never be fulfilled without the talking.

"That's okay with me."

She didn't really pay too much attention to what they ate. She knew it was tasty and filling, and that the chips were crispy on the outside but buttery soft on the inside. She washed down the meal with one beer, then switched to water, because she didn't want to be even buzzed for the conversation that she was both dreading and anticipating. She helped Rory clear away the detritus of their meal, tidied the kitchen, and followed him into the living room to sit, wishing she hadn't finished the water so she'd have something to occupy her hands.

"I've already told you where I stand as far as us being together is concerned, Chrissy," Rory began, the earnestness in his tone letting her know just how serious he was being. "But I need to explain why I didn't fight for you before, because I want *you* to explain why you never called me back. Does that seem fair to you?"

She nodded. Somehow, her ability to speak had been stolen by his willingness to lay himself out there for her to see, to share all his secrets, just so she would have a reason to trust him, to share with him in equal measure. She understood what it took to trust like that, how much it cost, how deep the fear ran.

He inhaled deeply, then began. "Fifteen years ago, I was left standing at the altar by a woman I had thought loved me, a woman I had fallen for the very first day I met her." Chrissy's shocked gasp didn't slow the flow of his words. "I hadn't started the band as yet, but I'd been talking about it with her for months after we moved in together, while I was still playing with the pit orchestra in the theater company I worked for at the time."

She wanted to reach for him, to stroke his hands, to let him know she was so sorry that he had been hurt. But he didn't seem to be struggling with any pain, so she kept her hands in her lap and listened as he continued.

"After that, and especially when I was also on the outs with my father over my career choices, I decided I needed to simplify my life. Going forward, the most I wanted from any woman was sex.

If I felt randy enough, I'd take what was offered, as long as they understood it wasn't a permanent arrangement, that all I wanted was a hookup."

He dragged a hand over his face, which Chrissy noted had got a bit of color in it. Was he embarrassed? She supposed she could understand why he'd feel that way. Having to tell the woman he was pursuing that he'd been a randy playboy for years couldn't be easy, particularly since he was saying that he wanted more now. Could she trust him? He had to be praying that she would.

"I'm guessing I messed with that plan?" Time to add something other than silence to the conversation.

His smile was wry. "You did. I had been expecting a different outcome the night I met you, but I wasn't averse to taking you home and seeing if you would be willing, at some future date, to fill in the gap. I'm not proud of it, but that's the whole truth." He looked her square in the eye then, as if he needed her to see the honesty in his words. "I'm sorry, love. You are far more to me than I intended you to be."

She did reach out then. He needed something that only she could give him ... her forgiveness.

"I believe you, Rory. Apology accepted."

He squeezed her hand and held on when she made to pull away from him. She let him hold on. She needed to hold on as well, to be honest, because soon it would be her turn to bare her own humiliating truths to him.

"Initially, I told myself that the only reason I pursued you and asked you out was because I wanted you in my bed. But I knew, even back then, that I was lying. There was something about you that made you different, something that made me want you for more than a hookup. But I had sworn off more with any woman, so I couldn't admit that to myself. And when you ghosted me, I told myself it was for the best, that I had been right not to try for more with you, that I had had a lucky escape. I didn't plan for history to ever repeat itself where women were concerned. So I didn't call because I needed to prove to myself that I was right, that you meant nothing, that the feelings I was squashing with everything in me would pass."

At his raw words, competing emotions rose inside Chrissy, building like a raging inferno, out of control and spreading like a forest wildfire. She'd never had anything like the conversation she was currently in with anyone before. And no one had ever made her feel the way Rory was doing at the moment, like she was about to boil over with a myriad of emotions. She wanted to be witty and sophisticated, to manage the feelings with some kind of mature finesse.

"How's that working out for you?"

There. Who could want a more sophisticated, cool, unfazed response? But it was lies ... all lies. She was as far from cool as she could be.

"You know how." His voice had taken on the quality of a rusty saw against an even rustier nail.

Suddenly he was pulling her against him, dragging her over his lap, wrapping his arms around her. But he kept his body painfully still, and he did not kiss her. She felt him under her thighs, in the soft place where they met ... hard, wanting, poised for action. But he didn't move, just waited for her to speak.

She instinctively recognized it as a power play on his part. She couldn't prevaricate when the evidence of his desire for her was waiting like a hungry lion to pounce if she made a move. She also understood, though, that rather than trying to manipulate her, he was putting her on notice regarding his true feelings, and also that she had the power of rejection over him, that he would be broken if she refused him.

Not that she planned to do any such thing. That would be like cutting off her nose to spite her face, and she might be a bit of an innocent in the ways of the world, but she was no fool. The nuns had taught her to use the common sense she'd been born with, and if she wanted to keep Rory, she had to begin with her own truth, as he had requested. But some instinct told her he needed reassurance, before she began, that what she had to say would not mean an end, but rather a continuation. So she did what came instinctively. She kissed him.

It was a chaste kiss, just a press of their lips together. But she knew he'd understand. She felt his arms tighten around her, but he held back from deepening it, and when she moved away to speak, he didn't follow. She appreciated his restraint. It would be so easy to lose herself and hide in the desire that had dogged her for a whole excruciating week without him. He had wakened a thirst she only knew and only wanted to quench with him. But *that* Chrissy—the one who ran away from her feelings, who let her fears rule her—was gone, and the new woman who had emerged from the shell of that old one was not going back in.

"The paparazzi and the fans spooked me that night after the concert, but that was really the last straw. I'd been on the verge of running for a while before that."

She took a huge breath, because despite her newfound need to be stronger and better than she'd been so far, opening up was scary. What if her ugly truth was worse than his? Would he forgive her as quickly and easily as she'd forgiven him?

"Chrissy, sweetheart, nothing you can tell me will change how I feel. I promise you. Will you tell me the rest, please, love?"

Oh, yeah, she'd forgotten that he was some kind of mind reader as well.

"I was really drawn to you from the night of my birthday party. I'm glad you didn't notice how I couldn't keep my eyes off you, though I did try, especially after I knew you'd come as Toni's plus-one. So I was really shocked when she asked you to take me home, and even more so when you agreed and didn't seem upset."

She chuckled as she remembered how nervous she'd been sitting in his car as he drove her home, and how she'd worked hard to keep her secret delight to herself. She was not about to give away how much she had liked having him to herself, especially since he hadn't seemed to be affected by her at all.

"Then you asked me out, more than once, to my shock and amazement, and it was clear that we had great chemistry." Those make-out sessions had been heart-stopping and overwhelming for her. "I stalked your social media to learn everything I could about you, and I kept wondering when you'd realize I wasn't the svelte, sexy, confident woman you were accustomed to taking on dates. Then you invited me to that concert, and I saw the way the groupies were with you. That just told me I didn't belong with someone like you. I was out of my element."

That wasn't something she liked to admit. It was one thing to know she was out of her league with Rory. It was another thing altogether to speak that truth aloud. That made it even more true, if that were possible.

"It didn't seem to bother you that random strangers were constantly trying to touch you and would do anything to get your hands on them, including baring their bodies to you in public. I didn't like any part of that, and I didn't feel good about being upset with you over something you clearly had no problem with. It wasn't my right."

"Chrissy..." he started, but she stopped him with a finger to his lips.

"No, let me finish. This is hard enough without you trying to be nice to me." He kissed her silencing finger and nodded. "I used that episode with the bare-breasted fan as an excuse to leave before you had a chance to send me away. I was too afraid to face even the possibility of your rejection, so I did it for you. And I didn't call because I was sure that *you* wouldn't, thus proving that I was right about you after all. Then I could move on with a clear conscience."

The hardest part was yet to be said, but it had to be. She had to clear the air completely, to get them onto a surer, stronger footing. But before she could continue, he asked, amusement lacing his voice, "How's that working out for you?"

She couldn't help but smile as he echoed her question from earlier.

"I really don't like the limelight, Rory, but I'm not stupid. I know it's a part of your life that I can't avoid. I knew it then too, but I wasn't ready to deal with it." She braced herself for the inevitable question that would require her to say the words her former self had refused to even acknowledge.

"And now you are?"

"Yes."

"Why now, love? What's changed?"

"I finally figured out that what I was really afraid of was intimacy." She looked him in the eye then, needing him to understand her. "I had never been with a man, and the desires you stirred up in me made me feel out of all control. I needed to keep control to protect myself from you. I couldn't let you have that much power over me."

"And now?"

Chrissy sighed. He wasn't going to let her get away with talking around it. "Now that I know what it feels like, what it can be when you're with someone who puts you first, I need to give this a chance, to prove to myself that I'm stronger and braver than the person I was seven months ago. That I'm someone you *can* be with. That I deserve to be with someone like you. That I am worth your time."

If she hadn't been looking into them, Chrissy would never have believed it could happen, but Rory's eyes darkened almost to purple, his face flushed with color, and his voice, when he spoke, was as dark as his eyes.

"Thank fuck! I'm glad we're on the same page at last, little kitten."

He kissed her then, long and slow and tender, but with the promise of a passion to be unleashed at their leisure. Now that they admitted to wanting the same thing with each other, they had time to talk about the rest. She had so many questions and concerns ... how to handle the paparazzi at work, how to stop them from invading her privacy at home, how to protect her aunts from unwanted publicity, how to keep her life story private. He must surely have a team to handle that, one that included a lawyer, should there be a need for legal measures to be taken.

"Hey." Rory's voice brought her out of her head. "Whatever it is you're thinking about, let it go. We will deal with all your questions tomorrow, hmm?" When she nodded, he continued. "For now, I'm in the mood to celebrate. Care to join me?"

"How exactly will we be celebrating?" She thought she knew, but she wanted him to say the words, to tease her with the promise of more.

He didn't answer her with words at first, just pushed his hips up against her hard, making her gasp. Then he said, "We can start here." He kissed her hungrily. "And then go where the spirit moves us."

She didn't have a problem with that.

Eventually, of course, they had to come up for air. On Saturday morning, Chrissy stole out of bed, taking a last longing look at the golden-haired man still sound asleep on his belly under her covers before heading to the kitchen to make tea. They hadn't slept much the night before, but she wasn't about to complain that she was exhausted or about the orgasms he had given her. Instead, she chose to sort out her thoughts over a cup of tea, because she needed a plan for the way her life was already changing, and Rory knew better than anyone else she knew how to do that.

Her cellphone pinged a message from Toni. But when she opened it, instead of Toni's words, there was a link to an online gossip column in a popular tabloid. Trepidation filled her, but she clicked on it, and read the headline: "Riordan, world-class rocker, slumming it with lowly secretary from Ely." There was a picture of the front of her flat as well as the ones already making the rounds on social media.

She threw the phone down on the counter and hung her head, holding back the tears. Was nowhere sacred? Strong hands on her shoulders eased the tension in them for a moment, until Rory asked, "What's happened, love?"

She showed him the phone, heard him swearing, and saw the anger on his face through a haze of tears. Then he turned those eyes to her fully, and she saw caution, as well.

"Are you ... what do you want to do?"

She sighed heavily, wiping her tears. "I don't know. What *can* we do?"

Light brightened the heaviness in his eyes. "I'll make some calls and get some things sorted. Do you want to stay here, or do you want to go somewhere else?"

She appreciated him giving her the choice, but this time, she'd let him decide. It was the best thing to do.

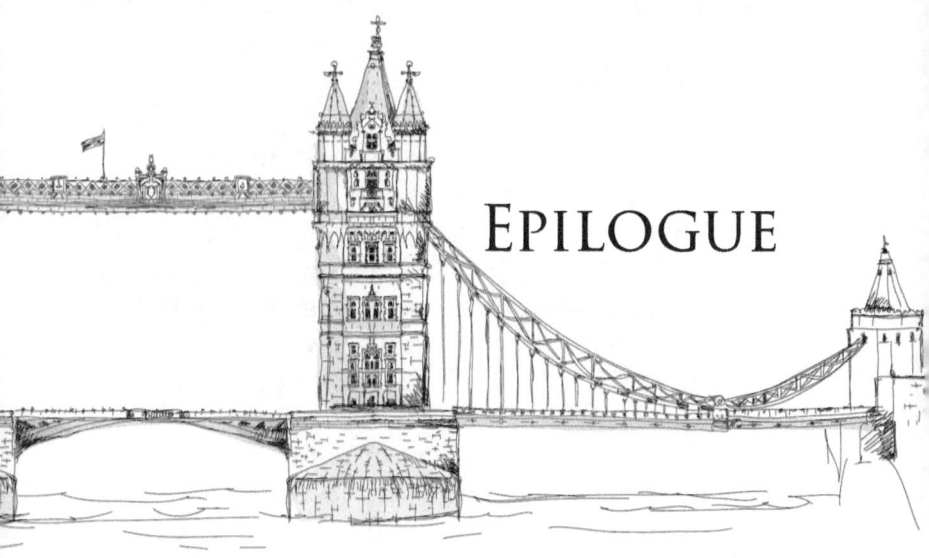

EPILOGUE

Where the devil is Rory? Chrissy checked the time again. It was almost seven, and he was supposed to have arrived fifteen minutes ago. Rory was never late, and he always announced his arrival with a phone call at least five minutes before. Had something happened? Had he been in an accident? Surely someone would have notified her by now if he had been?

Toni and Niall had invited them over for dinner with Karen and Peter, who were visiting from their home in The Netherlands. Rory had insisted on picking her up, because the last set of pictures of them after his last show in New York City had been much too close to home. Rory was very protective of her and had been since those first pictures of her flat had made it into the tabloids all those months ago.

She had been so tempted to run again, especially because it was clear that someone had followed her home. There was just no other way they could have got that photo. She'd panicked.

"What other pictures have they taken, Rory? Am I going to see my face next as I'm doing my supermarket shopping? And what if they follow me home to my aunts? I can't have that!"

"I promise you we'll take care of it, Chrissy. Trust me?"

That had been the first of many tests for the two of them. Rory understood the realities of fame, and she would have to trust him to take care of her and protect her from the worst of it. But she hated having to live like that, always watching out for who was watching her, having to check on her aunts constantly to make sure they weren't being harassed, worrying that someone some-where would pay the right amount of money for the story of her life.

She wasn't ashamed of who she was, but not knowing her parents, being a foundling, still stung. She understood that a part of the reason she had difficulty trusting anyone was that under-lying knowledge that the people who *should* have wanted her either hadn't or couldn't for some reason she would never know. She didn't want that to be put out there for public consumption. It was *her* business, no one else's.

She had not asked too many questions about what Rory did to keep her as publicity-free as she had managed to be. She knew that the board of directors at Hope House had made some kind of arrangement with his team that made it so the media did not hang around her place of work. But no one could stop them from following her or stalking her and Rory when they were out together. He'd even stopped driving his car, because they were relentless.

Why was the life of a rockstar suddenly so newsworthy? It wasn't as though he was into drugs or anything else illegal. She'd thought that with all the other celebrity news, she and Rory would become old hat, but for whatever reason, a few diehards kept bringing them back into focus every few months. It was disconcerting and frustrating.

She sighed, resisting the urge to check the time yet again. It wasn't as though Niall or Toni would mind if they weren't exactly on time, but she hated being late as much as Rory did. Pickles tried to climb onto her lap, trying for a head rub and some cuddles.

"Sorry, little kitty, but I need to be fur-free for dinner this evening. Come on, let's give you a treat before I go. Where's your brother?"

Her cellphone rang just as she reached for the bag. "This is Chrissy," she said, pulling out a couple of cat snacks.

"Sweetheart, I'm so sorry I'm late. I had a hold up at the studio. I'll be there in five."

"Okay. I'm glad you're okay. I was worried."

"I'm sorry I worried you, love. Be there soon."

She was waiting at the door when he knocked. She opened it and stepped out, into his arms. They had learned to restrict their PDAs to places where no one would take advantage, so he only smiled at her and walked with her to the limo. Once inside, behind the tinted windows, he leaned in and captured her lips.

"Hi. You're looking lovely as always."

"Thank you. You're looking ... tense." She took a moment to observe his face. "Is everything alright?"

"Everything's fine. I don't like being late, that's all. And we have to stop at my place before we go. I need to pick up a package that was delivered today that I have to take with me to Niall's."

Over the last few months, Chrissy had learned to trust her Spidey senses, as she called them, where Rory was concerned, and she could tell that he was hiding something. She didn't know what it was and couldn't even guess, but she knew that if it was another story in the tabloids or on social media, he'd have told her at once. That was one of the things they had agreed to when she first decided that she wanted to be with him more than she hated to be in the spotlight.

"I'll just let Toni know," she said, reaching for the phone in her clutch purse and choosing not to call him on her suspicion.

Rory forestalled her. "It's okay, I've already called them. I did right after I called you."

She narrowed her eyes at him but said nothing more, relaxing against him when he drew her close. She was sure she'd find out what he was hiding from her when he was ready to tell her. They had also agreed not to keep secrets from each other, no matter what, and so far, that had worked out well for them. So until he was ready, she wouldn't worry about it.

His house was dark when they arrived, and he urged her to go inside with him, "So I can steal a few proper kisses," he told her with a mischievous grin. Who was she to refuse such a tempting offer?

"As long as you don't try anything more," she said, wagging a finger at him.

He laughed. "Would I? Would I?"

She echoed his amusement. "We both know the answer to that is yes, you would."

The house was almost eerily quiet when they walked in. He switched on a light and turned to her.

"I asked my housekeeper to put it in the kitchen for me. Have a seat in the drawing room while I fetch it."

Chrissy nodded. She loved his drawing room with its elegant grand piano, the high-backed chairs and deep sofas, the beautiful artwork on the walls, and the gorgeous Persian rug that took up most of the floor space. She hit the light switch by the door as she walked in and almost fell over.

"Surprise!"

Chrissy blinked, her heart hammering wildly at the shock of seeing about twenty people all grinning at her. What the...?

"Rory!" she yelled, turning to find him standing right behind her, the biggest grin of all on his face.

"Surprise, little kitten!" He leaned in and kissed her cheek.

"What? Why?" She was truly confused.

"It's your birthday, love. How could you forget?"

Her eyes widened as a fresh suspicion rose in her mind. "What are you going to do that you haven't already done, Rory?" she asked, managing to keep the trepidation out of her voice.

She knew everyone in the room, most of whom had been at the first birthday party Toni had thrown for her. Still, she hadn't really expected anything more than the card she'd received from her aunts with a cheque for a hundred pounds— "Buy yourself some pretty things," the card said —the cake at work and the silliness at lunchtime, and the dinner party that Toni had planned. Toni ... she turned to look at her friend, who was still grinning like a Cheshire cat.

"So this is the dinner party you planned?" she asked, advancing to hug her.

"I haven't planned a thing, love. This is all Rory."

She turned back to the man she loved with a frown. "Did you even go upstairs to get the package?"

He shook his head, smiling tenderly at her as he came to stand in front of her. "I didn't need to. I've been carrying it around for weeks, waiting for tonight."

Her frown deepened just before comprehension dawned. The only thing she could think of that he could carry around on his person was...

"Rory?" She could feel the blood rushing through her body, increasing her heart rate and coloring her cheeks.

"Happy birthday, Chrissy," he said, pulling a long black box from his pocket and opening it so she could see what was inside.

It was a beautiful tennis bracelet, bestudded with her birthstone of brilliant sapphires, linked together by tiny diamonds.

"Oh my! Rory, it's gorgeous! Thank you so much."

She reached up to cup his cheeks then extended her hand so he could put it on. Then she turned to show it off to her friends, suppressing the little shot of disappointment that the gift hadn't been what she'd thought it was. They'd only known each other a year, after all. Why would he be proposing to her already? He wouldn't want to make the same mistake twice, and she knew what he felt about his first proposal. She ignored the little voice that said he was older and wiser, and he knew how she felt about him.

Suddenly noticing how quiet it had gone in the room, she turned around again to ask Rory what was happening and found him down on one knee, holding open a smaller black box with a complementary ring glittering in its center. The large marquis diamond, surrounded by bright sapphires, sparkled invitingly.

"We've only known each other a year, love," he began, holding her gaze, "and there are a lot of things I don't know about you, like your favorite color or your favorite book. I don't know what your dream job is or whether you only like cats. I don't even know where you went to school. But the things I do know are so precious to me that I want to keep them with me. Which means I need to keep you."

Chuckles sounded around the room for a moment before silence fell again. Chrissy couldn't take her eyes off the man kneeling at her feet.

"I love that you are warm and open, that you're loyal, fiercely protective, and kind to animals. I love your undying respect for your aunts. You understand the value of family, and you encourage me to be a better son. I love your diligence, your attention to detail, your sense of style, your appreciation of beautiful things, your love of simplicity. I love that you're brave yet cautious, humble and modest, yet honest to a fault. Honestly, I love everything about you."

He took her hand in his, kissing the back of it briefly before adding, "I've never met another woman like you. Will you be mine today and forever?"

Someone cued the song he'd written about his parents, "Forever And A Day," as Rory asked his question and the lyrics filled the silent space between them until she said, "Yes!" and he surged to his feet to wrap her in his arms and kiss her. She could feel the tension in his body as he held himself back from deepening the kiss. Then he took her hand and slid the ring onto the third finger, shoving the box into his pocket and pulling her back into his arms.

"I love you, Christina Marcus. Forever and a day."

THE END

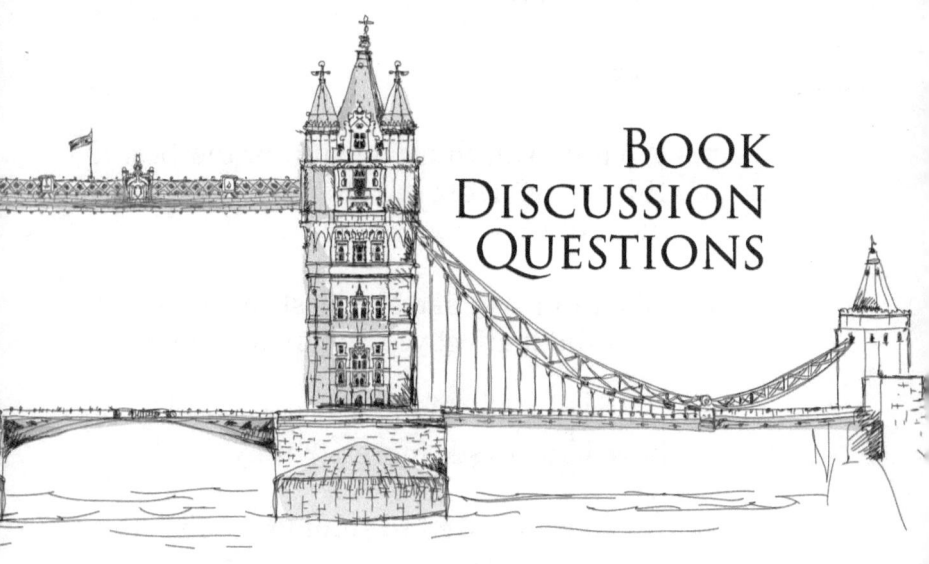

BOOK DISCUSSION QUESTIONS

1. What did you like most about Chrissy and Rory? Why?

2. What did you dislike most about them? Why?

3. If you were in Chrissy's position, how would you have reacted to the media scrutiny?

4. In what way(s) are Chrissy and Rory alike?

5. Which of them do you relate to the most? In what way(s)?

6. If this book were made into a movie, who would play Chrissy and Rory?

7. What do you think the author did best in this story? How did it affect your enjoyment of it?

8. What did you like the least in this story? How did it affect your enjoyment of it?

9. Which secondary characters would you have liked to see more of? Why?

10. If you were asked to summarize the story, what would be your talking points?

11. What passages or quotations stood out for you the most? Why?

12. How did the author convey the messages that you found most significant in this story?

13. If you could add anything to the story, where would you add it, and what would it be?

14. If you could ask the author any question about the book, what would it be?

K.T. BOND

KT Bond is an emerging author of contemporary romance across many subgenres. This Halloween baby likes to think the seed for romance writing was planted in her soul way back when she was a preteen reading Janet Daley, Betty Neels, Barbara Cartland, and Georgette Heyer. More than seven years ago, she started her second career as a ghostwriter of sweet and erotic romances. Now she writes stories for her own readers, using that experience and her greatly enlarged library of authors to show her the way forward. Life is filled with love stories waiting to be told, and she's excited to be able to share the joy of love with you, one story at a time.

Among other things, KT is a retired English educator, an avid reader, Nana to a sweet little Japanese-Jamaican girl, and the chief cook and dog walker in her family. She is a proud member of the renewed Romance Writers of America. This is the third and final book in the *Serendipity* series, which is all about second chances for older adults—a favorite subject of hers —and KT's eleventh book in her own name.

SOCIAL MEDIA

https://linktr.ee/kdjb

More books from
4 Horsemen Publications

Romance

Ann Shepphird
The War Council

Emily Bunney
All or Nothing
All the Way
All Night Long: Novella
All She Needs
Having it All
All at Once
All Together
All for Her

KT Bond
Back to Life
Back to Love
Back at Last

Lynn Chantale
The Baker's Touch
Blind Secrets
Broken Lens
Blind Fury
Time Bomb
VIP's Revenge
Chef's Taste

Mandy Fate
Love Me, Goaltender
Captain of My Heart

Mimi Francis
Private Lives
Private Protection
Private Party
Run Away Home
The Professor
Our Two-Week, One-
Night Stand

Shae Coon
Bound in Love
Controlling Assets
For His Own Protection
Her Broken Pieces
The Roma's Claim
The Roma's Promise

Discover more at
4HorsemenPublications.com

www.ingramcontent.com/pod-product-compliance
Lightning Source LLC
Chambersburg PA
CBHW020133120726
47903CB00007B/2234